The Dreams of Benjamin Pringle – Book

Wyldewych

M.P. Foxx

Best wishes
MPFoxx
x

Copyright Page

*This book is dedicated to all the children who read and enjoy
the story I have to tell, but specifically:*

*The two I call mine,
The one from another, but who read this first,
And the two who share what was once my name.*

'He had no beauty or majesty to attract us to him, nothing in his appearance that we should desire him.'

-Isaiah 53:2

1

Every Tree Will Bow

'Don't be a fool, boy,' said the man. 'Give it to me.'

'I – I can't breathe - it's burning,' Benjamin coughed and put his hands to his throat. The figure came towards him and Benjamin strained to see his face through the thick dust.

'It's over,' the mysterious figure said. 'He's dead.'

'No!' Benjamin cried. He turned and ran towards the door at the end of the dark tunnel. A dim light shone through the cracks in the door. The man's footsteps were close behind him. Benjamin ran faster, the pendant around his neck beating softly against his chest. As the door got closer, he held out his hand to grasp the handle. With inches left he tripped and began to fall.

Benjamin jerked awake. He sat up and looked around his dark bedroom, the dream still fresh in his memory.

'Not again,' he said softly to himself and lay back down.

Tossing and turning, he tried to get back to sleep, but the dream was waiting for him every time he closed his eyes. He gave up, and his legs trembled as he climbed down off the top bunk. Riley, the housemate who shared the bedroom, stirred when the ladder creaked. Benjamin looked blankly at Riley as questions popped in to his head. Who was the man with no face? What did he want? Most importantly, who was dead? Always the same dream, he thought, but never any answers.

Thoughts plagued him as he peered out of his room and looked longingly down the corridor. He wished his parents were in one of the other bedrooms, but instead were two boys who slept in those rooms. They lived with him and Riley at Hadley Priest Children's Home.

Small for his age, Benjamin crept down the bare wooden stairs silently, pausing twice to glance over his shoulder. Once at the bottom, he scurried across the house into the sparsely furnished front room. He took his usual seat by the front window, the broken chair's springs aching even under his slender frame. As he sat down, the familiar smell of musty cushion and mothballs, found his nose. Outside, the street lights burned dully through the fog, bringing some welcome light. Benjamin sat, his eyes fixed on the street light, gripping the arms of the chair and jumping at every creak the house made.

To distract himself, Benjamin picked out the brightest stars twinkling in the sky. He closed his eyes and made a wish. Not that it'll ever come true, he thought to himself. I'll be stuck here forever.

Morning came and rain flecked the window of the front room. From Benjamin's breath a patch of fog grew on the glass, and he drew a frowning face in it. His blue eyes watched people pass by outside; children splashed in the puddles as adults hurried them along, shielding themselves from the rain. A soft thump at the bottom of the stairs made Benjamin turn his head. Marcus Ferguson stood tall in the doorway, his hands in his pockets.

'Can't sleep?' Marcus asked. His pale skin shone in the early morning light. Dotted with freckles and topped with a head of curly red hair, Marcus was taller and older than Benjamin.

Benjamin nodded. 'Bad dream.'

'The one about the dead bloke?' Marcus asked.

'Yeah.'

Marcus reached for his rucksack on the floor. 'You don't need any more of them,' he said with a scowl and looked around. 'Living here *is* a bad dream.'

Benjamin nodded again and noticed that Marcus had his school uniform on. 'You're leaving early.'

'Detention.' Marcus rolled his eyes and pretended to play with loose change in his trouser pocket.

Benjamin smirked. 'What did you do this time?'

'Well, let's just say the science lab will never be the same again.' Benjamin and Marcus looked at each other and chuckled silently.

They watched the postman walk by the window. 'No post?' Marcus asked half-heartedly.

Benjamin looked at him. 'We never get post. Well, at least not since I've lived here.'

'All of ten years,' Marcus teased. 'Maybe Hester the Humungous eats the post before we see it.' Benjamin looked at him in disbelief.

'I'm joking.'

Marcus turned to leave and stepped on a creaky floor board. A loud snort came from behind the closed bedroom door of the House Matron, Hester Troggs.

'Shh!' Benjamin pressed his finger to his lips. 'I don't need her out here.'

Marcus scoffed. 'You think that will wake her up? She's so lazy she wouldn't get out of bed if the house was burning to the ground.'

Benjamin stifled a laugh. 'You should get going. If she finds out you've got detention again, she'll go mental.'

'What's new? See ya.'

'See ya.'

The front door closed lightly. The wind whistled through the gaps between the window and the house. Shaking off the dream, Benjamin sighed and turned his head towards the simple square clock that hung crookedly on the wall. 'My turn,' he said reluctantly. He got dressed as quietly as possible and started out for school.

He closed the door behind him with one hand, the other one cradling a peanut butter sandwich. He took a bite and looked at the outside of the house. It was almost invisible; no one ever seemed to notice it crammed between the others on the street. With its faded red door and peeling, yellowish-white paint, it looked very different from the rest of the houses, and still no one ever took any notice. Marcus called it the invisible cave. He would always say, 'We're the only ones that know this place even exists. Must be a curse or something.'

Benjamin studied the outside for a moment longer. Whatever had been on the tarnished bronze plaque that hung by the door had worn off. He looked towards the road at the neighbours walking by. Their houses looked much nicer.

He stuffed the last of the sandwich into his mouth and ran his hands through his dirty blond hair before slinging his rucksack over his worn out clothes. The soles of his shoes made a flipping sound as he walked down the street and up the alley towards his school.

Benjamin was soon lost in thought about school and what had happened to him the day before.

'Where's your family photo, Pringle?' The class bully, Huxley Boyd, had waited until the entire class filed in before asking. 'Yours is the only one missing.' His voice grew louder and a few of Huxley's mates that had gathered around chuckled as Benjamin sat down.

His feet shifted under his desk. 'I don't – I don't have one.' Benjamin's eyes never left the floor. He could hear his classmates whispering all around him.

But now, as he walked up the path, it was a different whisper that Benjamin heard, and it was enough to bring him out of one of his many bad memories. His eyes scanned the small trees that dotted the edge of the alley. They stood like mini soldiers in the autumn drizzle, bare of all their leaves. Although there was nobody else around, Benjamin was convinced he heard voices.

Determined not to look up, Benjamin put his head down and quickened his pace. Maybe for Benjamin that was just as well, because if he had looked up he would have seen the trees bow down after him.

2

The Sliding Stairs

The house was quiet when Benjamin got back from school. He dropped his rucksack and tried to forget one of the worst days he had ever had. The day had begun with him being the only one not chosen for football in PE, and ended with Huxley Boyd and his mates throwing him in to the skip at the bottom of the alley on his way home. As a result, Benjamin walked the rest of the way home dragging his rucksack and smelling like rubbish.

'Yuk! I can smell you from here.' Marcus crinkled his nose up and fanned his hand in front of him as he came down the stairs. He studied Benjamin's messed up hair and rubbish stained shirt. 'Rough day?'

'You could say that.' Benjamin went into the kitchen and put his mouth under the tap to get a drink of water. He went to pull the fridge door open but it was locked. 'How could I forget,' he said irritably and leant against one of the many dirty walls.

'The old bat changed the locks again, it'll take me a minute to figure it out,' Marcus said. He followed Benjamin into the kitchen, walking by the only picture in the whole house. It was a portrait of a man with a blurred face. The writing on the bottom read, *Hadley Priest, 1848-1903. Philanthropist and father to all.*

'Where's Hester?' Benjamin asked.

'Who cares,' responded Marcus. 'She's never around, is she?'

Benjamin shrugged. 'Gives you more time to break in to all the locked doors then, doesn't it?' Sitting underneath the stairs, the cellar door caught Benjamin's eye. 'Except one,' he said softly.

Unlike the dilapidated state of the rest of the house, the cellar door's thick wood panels were solid and unscathed, with a brass doorknob that sat over a keyhole of almost the same size. It was always locked and the doorknob didn't turn. Benjamin had once seen Hester try to unlock it without any luck.

He thought back to that night. He had been woken up by noises from below his room, and crept down to see Hester in front of the cellar door trying to unlock it. One by one she had tried every key on her belt, jamming and wriggling them, but the door didn't budge. Suddenly there was a flash of light from behind the door and Hester was sent flying into the wall on the other side of the corridor. Benjamin had run back upstairs and woken Marcus.

'No way,' Marcus had said. 'Hester weighs a ton, there's no way she got thrown off her feet.'

'I swear.' Benjamin remembered feeling prickly all over. 'I saw it with my own eyes.' Marcus had made Benjamin cross his heart.

'We'll wait until she goes to bed and then get her keys. I'll get that door open.'

After two games of snap by torchlight Marcus had stood up. 'Let's go.'

'How are you going to get the keys?' Benjamin had tried to sound confident as they went downstairs. Marcus had scoffed.

'She sleeps like a log. It'll be easy.' And within seconds, Marcus had crept out of Hester's room, his hands wrapped around a big bunch of keys. 'Stand clear.' He turned to Benjamin. 'I wouldn't want you to get hurt.' The mocking in Marcus' voice had stung Benjamin. Marcus was thrown back after only the second key.

'This whole house creeps me out,' he had said after picking himself up.

Benjamin had taken cover in his bed and had kept clear of the door ever since.

'Benjamin. Benjamin.'

'Hey! Bin Boy.' A slight poke on his shoulder snapped Benjamin out of his daze. He turned to see Marcus with the fridge open, a smile on his face and a paperclip in his hand. 'Dig in.'

Their feast was interrupted by a thud upstairs, followed by a shout from Hester.

'I knew you were up to something!'

Benjamin and Marcus stuffed what they could in their mouths and went towards the bottom of the stairs. The next thing they heard was little Riley's voice coming from his bedroom.

'But I don't like spiders,' Riley pleaded. 'They're just waiting for me to fall asleep so they can make nests in my ears.'

'You're always up to no good, you are. All these contraptions you make.' Hester's voice was getting louder and higher with every breath she took.

'They're bug traps. I don't like bugs.' Riley's voice tailed off.

'Afraid of bugs. Nests in your ears. I've never heard such nonsense. All those ears need is a good tug!' Hester hollered. 'I should throw you outside. A good dose of the back garden will fix you. You can trap all the bugs you want.'

'No, I don't want to go. It's a jungle back there and the newts will eat the skin off the tips of my toes.'

Marcus and Benjamin stood at the bottom of the stairs, looking up to where the voices were coming from.

'She's gonna throw him in the jungle.' Marcus gulped down his last mouthful of food and looked at Benjamin.

'No way, he's only five. Ah!' Benjamin bit his tongue. 'Some of the weeds are taller than him. Not to mention all the rubbish.'

'Wanna bet?'

'Marcus, there's probably rats the size of cats back there. Remember when Motley made us catch rats for him once in that garden? She's having a laugh.'

'Her lips were not made for smiling.'

Benjamin shook his head.

'Mate, Hester the Horrible does what she wants.'

'Someone's got to stop her.'

Marcus raised his eyebrows. 'Who? You?'

'Maybe,' said Benjamin under his breath.

Hester led Riley down the stairs by his left ear. Her huge body towered over Riley, with his straight blond hair and brown eyes. His glasses were perched crookedly on his nose.

'Ouch! You're hurting me.' Riley winced.

'You're lucky this be all that I'm doing to you.' She shot back. 'Move!' She brushed past Marcus and Benjamin. Benjamin found his voice.

'Leave him alone.'

Slowly, Hester turned to face him, a shocked look on her face. Riley used the opportunity to wriggle free and scamper up the stairs.

'What did you say to me?' Her voice was low and threatening. She walked slowly towards Benjamin until she was almost on top of him.

Benjamin struggled to speak. 'Leave him alone.' His hands had formed tight fists at either side of his body but his eyes struggled to meet hers.

'Oh!' Hester straightened up. 'And what are you going to do about it?' Her eyebrows curled towards the middle of her forehead. 'Speak up.' She shot back, her eyes fixed on him.

Benjamin stood there, unable to answer. His fists shaking slightly, he wanted to reach out and punch her in the nose.

'I'll clean up the mess I made in my room,' said Riley desperately from the top of the stairs.

Hester turned to look at him. 'Yes you will, once I'm finished with you.' She heaved her massive body up the stairs. Riley's eyes widened.

'I said leave him alone.' Benjamin could hear the words come out of his mouth. He reached out his hand to hold Hester back but he missed – or so he thought.

Instantly, Hester dropped as the stairs beneath her feet flattened and turned in to a slide. From half-way up, she slid down on her belly to where Benjamin was standing at the bottom. Marcus held back a laugh, but the other two were dumbstruck.

Hester got up and looked at Benjamin with a mixture of confusion, fear and disdain on her face. 'How? How did you - '

'I didn't do anything, I swear.' Benjamin took a few steps back.

Hester turned to look at the stairs, which had gone back to their normal state. Her eyes flashed back to Benjamin. 'That's the work of the devil, that is.' She pointed to him. 'It's you. You're the devil in disguise!'

'No he's not! It's this creepy house, not him. Isn't it?' Marcus looked over to Benjamin who managed a small nod.

Hester struggled to find her balance. Marcus could hold back no longer and his shoulders began to shake with laughter. He squeezed his lips together with his fingers to force back a smile.

But Hester didn't hear what Marcus had said, nor did she notice what he was doing. She only had eyes for Benjamin, who by this time had backed himself into a corner by the front door. He never took his eyes off Hester, his mind bursting with thoughts of what she was going to do to him. They stood staring at each other for a few moments.

'I need a drink.' Hester broke the thick silence and stumbled out the front door, her eyes cast downwards.

Benjamin came out of the corner and tried not to look at Marcus or Riley.

'Mate!' Marcus said with a mixture of shock and admiration.

'I had nothing to do with it.' Benjamin tried to sound convinced.

Marcus shrugged. 'Well, however it happened, it was brilliant. Creepy, but brilliant.'

A few hours later Benjamin was at the kitchen table pouring over his homework, trying to get the stair episode out of his mind. Dried out brown beans dotted the dirty plates opposite him. Marcus came down the stairs with a pair of crusty old socks. 'Those are minging,' he said as he held them out at arms' length, walking towards the bin.

Benjamin held his nose. 'Whose are they?'

'Who do you think?' Marcus dropped them in to the bin. 'Riley told me they got stuck on the floor when Hester caught him putting glue in front of the bed – '

' – to stop the spiders.' Benjamin finished.

Marcus nodded. 'Well, Riley said that after those minging socks got stuck, she fell.'

'So that was the thud.'

'Must have been, but I'm surprised she didn't come right through the floor.' Marcus chuckled. 'Anyway, Riley said her glasses flew from the top of her head so I looked around and found them underneath the window.'

Marcus held up the small square reading glasses. They were streaked with sticky glue.

'How much glue is on the floor?' Benjamin asked.

'None now, but these, well,' he looked at the glasses, 'I may have helped them along.'

Benjamin shook his head. 'She's going to go mad.'

'It's all worth it, mate.' Marcus came up behind Benjamin and patted him on the shoulder. 'Watching her go mad is the reason I get up in the morning.'

'Yeah, well if I don't get this homework done I best just not show my face in school tomorrow. And I don't want to be around tonight when Motley decides to come back.'

'Yuh,' Marcus gave a shudder. 'That bloke is scary. Good thing he's hardly around. Where do you reckon he goes?'

'I don't know. It's spooky that he always knows what's going on around here. He could be in the walls for all we know.'

Marcus nodded. 'Remember the time he knew we had cut the toes out of Hester's stockings?"

'Yeah. He made us do stuff so he wouldn't tell, like catching those rats in the back garden for his pet snake he says he has in his room.'

'And then when I snuck into his room to try and find it, he said he saw me in his sleep.' Marcus shook his head. 'I swear he has see-through eyelids. He's mental, that one, barking mad.'

'Just talking about him gives me the creeps,' Benjamin agreed and twisted his pencil in his hand.

'I don't know why you're still freaked out by him,' Marcus said with a slight smile. 'Couldn't you just turn him into a toad or something?'

'How many times do I have to tell you, I didn't do anything to those stairs.' Benjamin leaned back in frustration. 'Why don't you believe me?'

'Okay, okay, I believe you. Whatever.' Marcus studied Benjamin's math and added in a few right answers. 'She probably did it herself. She could break an elephant's back, she could.'

Marcus yawned and handed Benjamin his pencil. 'Well, that's me done. Good night.' Marcus turned and headed upstairs. Benjamin gave a wave and stayed at the table for a while longer to struggle with his maths.

'You're up late.'

Benjamin jumped. He sensed the tall dark outline of Motley behind him.

'M-Motley. I didn't hear – didn't hear you come in.'

'That's good,' Motley answered in a cold, smooth voice. 'You never know where or when I could turn up.'

'I'll, uh. I'll keep that in mind.' Benjamin turned back to his homework, but he was hardly able to concentrate. He fingered the pages of his book and moved his eyes from side to side. He could feel Motley's eyes staring at him from under his black hat; he could hear him scarcely breathing.

Benjamin swallowed hard. 'Well, good night,' he said and closed his eyes tight. 'Please let him go anywhere but here,' he said under his breath.

'Sweet dreams. You never know, I might see you in them.' Motley slid away and moved silently up the stairs.

Benjamin sat motionless in his chair and waited until the coast was clear. He let out a sigh of relief and started packing up his unfinished homework, reasoning that the wrath of his teacher was better than meeting up with Motley or Hester again.

Once up in his room, Benjamin laid in bed shivering. The heating had been broken for a week. The house was quiet, save for the raspy snores of little Riley sprawled out under the thin covers, his arms over his head and his stuffed toy monkey, Doodle, between his feet. For the hundredth time Benjamin thought about Hester and the stairs.

How did that happen? There was no way he could have had anything to do with it. He closed his heavy eyelids and his thoughts switched to Motley. Maybe he *was* in the walls and he had made the stairs collapse. His thoughts were broken by the sounds of Riley snoring, it was getting further away.

Benjamin had a dream.

He dreamed he was downstairs looking out the front room window. … He was counting stars. … They soared towards him and through the glass, exploding into the cellar door. … Benjamin was at the door and read the message the stars left … *Once lost and now found, our search has come to ground. Through this door we bring you to a world where once you knew.* … The doorknob started to move and shake. …

…his dream changed…

…he turned around and saw Motley's face. His mouth open and his eyes flashing with anger… He pushed Benjamin aside and grasped the handle of the cellar door but it burned him. … Motley took his hand away and let out an ear-piercing scream …

Benjamin woke up with a start, covered in sweat despite the chill in the air. Over his shallow breathing he heard noises downstairs.

He crept down, his legs like jelly. On the last step he gasped and pressed his back into the wall. Motley was standing not more than six feet in front of him.

His head was turned away from Benjamin slightly and it seemed he hadn't heard him. He stood in front of the cellar door and studied it intently before he reached out to open it. With a slight hiss he pulled his hand back quickly and put two fingers in his mouth as a small puff of smoke rose from the doorknob.

Benjamin stood motionless, pressed against the wall in a pocket of darkness. His heart was pounding harder than usual.

Convinced his loud breathing would give him away, he braced himself but Motley went the other way.

As silently as he had come in earlier, Motley headed towards the front door. Benjamin watched as Motley walked right through the front door without opening it.

Benjamin forced a swallow down his dry throat and went over to the cellar door. It looked the same as always. As he turned to leave, the doorknob started to move and shake. He backed away, his eyes fixed on the door. His back met the wall across the corridor and he turned around, startled. The portrait hung crookedly just above him. The blurred face of Hadley Priest was moving. 'I'd open it if I were you,' the portrait said.

Benjamin backed up again and turned to face the door. It was rattling louder now, and the whole door was shaking. He took a deep breath, closed his eyes and wrapped his hand around the knob. The door sprang open. Benjamin looked down at the stairs that descended steeply into darkness.

'You!'

Benjamin looked to his left and saw Motley standing at the front door. For an instant both of them were frozen with surprise. Motley recovered first and advanced on Benjamin.

Benjamin's hair blew in the huge gust of wind that came up from the cellar and swirled around them. The open door started to close, pushing him closer towards the stairs. Before he could steady himself, he was thrown down in to the cellar, the door slamming shut behind him.

Inches away on the other side of the door, Motley clenched his outstretched hand into a fist and whispered, 'You won't get far.'

3

Dragon Scales, Hard as Nails

Benjamin tumbled down the stairs until he landed face first in a patch of soft, springy moss.

Standing up, he found he was in a small clearing surrounded by seven high stones planted in the ground. Next to Benjamin lay a flat stone marker. He brushed the grass and dirt from the marker, unable to make out the faded writing.

He looked around, bewildered. The muted sunlight that filtered through the huge trees made him blink. He was finding it hard to walk – as if the thick air was trying to hold him back. 'Everything's going crazy tonight,' he said out loud as he walked around the stone markers, exploring his new surroundings.

To Benjamin's right was a narrow path through the trees. He went towards it cautiously and gripped his churning stomach.

Ivy covered tree trunks lined the path that curved left and right; down small slopes and up small hills. As he walked, his thoughts drifted to his last dream. What did that message on the door mean? Once lost and now found? A world you knew? All around him huge leaves the colours of bronze and gold fell from the trees. When they touched the forest floor they vanished.

21

A horrible, raspy honking sound ahead made Benjamin jump. He dove behind a giant tree trunk, making sure he was fully hidden. After a few minutes of silence he started out again but retreated when the sound came back. This time it was closer and followed by a voice.

'C'mon, sweet'art, I knows ya gots it in ya. C'mon now, there's a good lass. Ya just need a little r'n'r, that's what I say.'

Benjamin pressed himself into the tree as hard as he could. His sweaty hands gripped the bark nervously and he struggled to balance on the slimy roots.

'Baawww.' The deep, raspy sound closed in.

'Awright, darlin', if ya say so, we'll try an' find it fer ya. But I still say it's trapped up inside ya, I do.'

Twigs crackled underneath heavy feet. Benjamin shot out from behind the tree towards the path he had just come from. As he did, his foot caught a root and he tripped. Flying head first into the path, he landed at the feet of the very thing he was trying to run away from.

'Aahh!'

'Aaahhhh!'

An odd-looking man stood directly in front of Benjamin. Startled at first, the man was now looking down at him with a smile on his face.

'Ya did give me a fright fer a moment there,' said the little man. He stretched out his hand to Benjamin. 'I mean, I was on me way ter meet ya but I certainly didn't expect ya ter fall out from behind a tree, no I didn't.'

Reluctantly, Benjamin took the man's hand and stood up, eye to eye with him. 'Excuse me, but did you just say you were coming to meet me?' Benjamin asked, bemused.

'Aye, so I was, but, as ya can see, I got a little behind me schedule.' The man rolled his eyes. 'I had a few wee problems along the way.' The man motioned his head over his shoulder but Benjamin couldn't see anything.

'Where's me manners?' sighed the little man, shaking his head. 'Jeems at yer service.' He doubled over in a low bow. His scruffy whiskers hid his oddly long but young looking face. His sandy brown hair was cut unevenly around his head – short at the back and long at the sides. He was dressed in funny green and tan clothes and wore a brown hat that was shaped like a pork pie. 'This 'ere's Primrose. She's me dragon.'

'Your dra-dragon?' Benjamin stammered and took a few steps back. He looked beyond Jeems but couldn't see anything. 'Where is it?' He asked, not sure he really wanted to know the answer.

'Well, she's right here behind me,' said Jeems, turning around. Jeems dropped his hands to his sides. 'Wha – Primrose! Get out 'ere! Come on out an' be friendly. We don't have time fer yer shenanigans, so we don't!'

A few moments later Primrose came out from behind the trees hesitantly, her hands over her eyes.

'Whoa,' said Benjamin.

'Ain't she a beauty?' Jeems smiled. Benjamin felt the blood drain from his face. 'Oh, don't ya worry 'bout her, she wouldn't hurt a flea. Well, not unless she got well bothered.' Jeems took Benjamin's arm to stop him from creeping behind another large tree. Benjamin blinked, unable to take his eyes off the dragon.

'Say allo, sweet'art,' Jeems said in a loving voice. 'Say allo ter – ter -,' Jeems turned to Benjamin, 'I'm sorry, we wasn't sure wot ya'd bin known as all these years. Wot did ya say yer name was?'

'Er – Benjamin.'

Jeems nodded and continued to coax his pet. 'Say allo ter Benjermin.'

Three thick purple fingers opened up over one eye, letting out a blinding light that made Benjamin stumble backwards.

Jeems steadied him. 'Her eyes get well bright when she has them covered up fer a bit. Should dull up in no time now.'

She stood at least the height of two men and was covered from head to toe in shimmering purple scales. Along her lower back and tail were thick, rounded iridescent spikes. Her underside was a goldish green and looked softer than her rock hard back shell. She had a very long, thick snout that was

24

partially covered by six thick purple fingers, three on each hand, which were connected to short, skinny arms.

'Well, don't be rude, darlin', say allo,' prompted Jeems again as the light faded.

Benjamin found his voice. 'Uh – I mean – it's okay if she doesn't want to. I – I don't mind. She looks n-nervous.'

'Nonsense,' scoffed Jeems. 'She's awright now, ain't ya, Primrose? Now that ya know this here little lad in't gonna hurt ya.' Jeems went over to Primrose and stroked her snout. Primrose immediately bent her head into Jeems. 'Go on now, say allo,' he coaxed quietly.

Primrose lifted her head slightly and opened her mouth. 'Baaww.'

'H-Hello,' answered Benjamin. He wasn't really sure what to say to a dragon.

'She's a grand girl, this one,' cooed Jeems, 'not half as big as most of 'em get. She must have been the runt or the like. She's not likely ter grow any more. Mind, she's big enough ter be scary.'

'You can say that again,' muttered Benjamin under his breath.

Jeems didn't appear to notice, but kept right on talking. 'She's the reason we're late. We was tryin' ter find her snuff, so we were. She reckons she lost it back in the muck pit when she scared off them forest rats with a wee spark or two.'

Benjamin's head was spinning. 'Wait - did you say spark? As in fire? Fir- oh – don't tell me she can breathe fire!' Benjamin stood with his mouth wide open. He knew that however he told it, Marcus and Riley would never believe him.

Jeems looked at Benjamin in disbelief. 'Well o' course she can breathe fire. Wot d'yer think a dragon's supposed ter do – play with leprechauns? She's a good little fire-breather, she is, when she gets her confidence up. Trouble is,' Jeems closed in on Benjamin, lowering his voice, 'she's gone an' convinced herself that she's lost it- calls it her snuff. She's got it in her, just thinks she don't. Thought I'd play along fer awhile, but then we was gettin' late so I had ter hurry her along.' Jeems straightened out and turned his attention back over to Primrose, who was catching odd-looking creatures just off the path and crunching them to bits.

It took Benjamin a moment to find his nerve. 'You said you were supposed to meet me. How did you know I was coming?'

'Well, I didn't at first. It was Gideon, so it was. He asked me ter meet ya.' Jeems straightened up with a sense of pride. 'Said he couldn't think of a better person ter welcome ya ter Meridia.'

'Meridia? And who's Gideon?'

'Now, there's a good question,' responded Jeems. 'Let's see, Gideon … well, Gideon is …l … well…' Jeems was thoughtful. 'I don't reckon I can really describe him. Ya'll have ter wait 'til ya meet him. That's the best way.'

Benjamin watched in disgust as Primrose bit off the head of a short cat-sized creature with a squished snout and ominous looking quills on its back.

'Them wurvils are tough li'l critters ter us, but right good eatin' fer our Primrose. Her teeth crunch right through them quills. Well, we best be goin'. Gideon is waitin' fer ya.' Jeems started to walk down the path before turning to look at Benjamin who hadn't moved. 'Are ya comin'?'

Benjamin felt dizzy with all of the questions he had, and was not sure about Meridia, or Jeems, and certainly not Primrose. But, he reasoned, anything was better than Hadley Priest, so he followed along.

The ground was bumpy, littered with exposed tree roots that grew across the path in a zigzag pattern. Benjamin kept his eyes on the ground. Jeems had said to keep on the path, so he didn't think tripping over another root was a good idea. They continued on until Jeems stopped abruptly.

'Ow.'

Benjamin, who hadn't noticed Jeems stop, bumped in to him, stepping on his toe. As Jeems gave Benjamin a scowl and rubbed his foot, the path ahead of them was swallowed by the trees on either side. Low-lying bushes spread across the path, their once soft leaves now sharp and unwelcoming. The tree trunks inflated and pushed up against each other. There was nowhere to go, the path was blocked.

'What happened?' Benjamin reached out to touch one of the trees but Jeems stopped him.

'Don' worry 'bout that. That there happens sometimes. Hasn't always been like it, but these days there's nothin' normal 'round here.' Jeems groaned as he sat down cross-legged on the path. 'Best just ter wait until it decides ter open up again.'

'How long will that take?'

Jeems shook his head slowly and shrugged his shoulders. 'Hard ter say. I've seen it open up as fast as it's closed, an' other times I've bin sat 'round fer close ter a day.'

'A day! What are we supposed to do now?'

'We wait,' Jeems said.

Sighing, Benjamin turned to examine the trees. The colours of the leaves had changed to very dark red and black. Like the leaves below, the trunks looked sharp and threatening.

Benjamin heard Primrose crunch up another creature. Looking away, he saw a small clearing he hadn't noticed before. 'We would have walked right by that,' he said to Jeems, approaching its edge.

'It wasn't there before,' remarked Jeems suspiciously.

Looking past the green, Benjamin saw their path carrying on, clearly marked.

'Look Jeems, we don't have to wait for the trees to open up. I can see the path across this green. All we've got to do is go across here and we'll be on the other side of these possessed trees.'

Jeems began shaking his head. 'No way, no how. Ya need ter stay on this path. That's a trick, that is. Ya never know wot's out there.'

Without waiting, Benjamin started through the green, the thick grass moist and lush against his shoes.

'Benjermin, come back! Don't go that way!' cried Jeems.

Suddenly the dim sunlight disappeared and Benjamin felt something move around his feet. The thick, soft blades of grass turned greenish grey with black warts. Their sharp points pierced his shoes like thick pins. Angry little faces wriggled from their flat edges. Benjamin felt a number of tiny but strong arms wrap around his ankles. They pulled themselves towards him, their mouths full of spiky, razor sharp teeth. They had nasty, hoarse voices which uttered only one word – '*narl.*'

'Help!' Benjamin screamed, struggling to free his feet. 'Help!'

'Hang on!' shouted Jeems from the path. 'Yer've been trapped by a load of furls.' Jeems looked around. 'Wot d'yer do 'bout furls?' he asked Primrose.

'Hurry.' Benjamin cried and kicked the creatures away as best he could. The furls tore away at the bottom of his trousers, eating each other without noticing.

At that moment Primrose bawled loudly, her thick scales glittering. 'Scales.' Jeems said. 'Dragon scales. Them furls'll never bite through them.' He jumped onto Primrose's back, his leg tearing on her thick, sharp scales.

'Quick, Primrose, we've gotta go an' git him!' Jeems urged her. Primrose backed away from the field, shaking her head.

'Ya've got ter,' said Jeems, egging her on. 'Yer the only one that can. They can't bite through yer skin, I know they can't.' Still Primrose hesitated.

'C'mon,' said Jeems again, more sternly this time. 'I promise, ya won't git hurt.'

She lurched into the field of swarming furls. Their sounds were deafening.

Benjamin struggled to stay standing. To his relief, Jeems and Primrose came alongside. 'Benjermin, take me hand,' yelled Jeems over the hum of the furls.

Benjamin reached out. They missed twice before their hands found each other. 'Got ya,' said Jeems, 'now just -'

'Oh no!' Benjamin cried as he fell backwards. Jeems lurched forward to catch him and slid off Primrose's neck.

'C'mon.' Jeems heaved Benjamin over his head seconds before falling from the dragon, his one arm wrapped tightly around her horns. Jeems struggled while Benjamin climbed on to Primrose's back. Almost instantly he felt his stomach scratch and tear from her sharp, rough scales.

'You can do it,' Benjamin turned to Jeems. He wanted to help but he was unable to move. He watched as Jeems struggled to clamber back on to Primrose, his hands cut and scratched. *Move,* Benjamin told himself. *Help him!* But it was too late. Jeems was pulled down as a furl sunk its teeth into his left leg.

'Jeems!' Without thinking, Benjamin lurched forward and grabbed Jeems' arm. 'I've got you.'

'Primrose, get us outta here.' Jeems was barely able to hold on. 'Hang on Benjermin.' He strained to speak. No sooner had Benjamin linked their arms then Primrose bounded out of the field. He jostled around on her back, bumping up, down and sideways. Feeling dizzy and sick, he closed his eyes, and somehow saw a scene unfold at Hadley Priest.

4

Grains of Sand

'Psst. Marcus, wake up.'

Marcus turned restlessly away from the gravelly whisper in his ear.

'Psst. Marcus, I mean it. You've got to wake up. Motley's gone mad.'

Marcus turned his head and forced his eyes open. Riley was standing beside his bed. His eyes, bloodshot and filled with fear were magnified from his thick glasses.

'Riley, it's the middle of the night, go back to sleep.' Marcus groaned, stretched under his thin blanket and yawned.

'I can't,' Riley replied hoarsely. 'Motley came in to my room.' Marcus propped himself up on his elbows. 'What for?'

'I don't know. But he was going through Benjamin's stuff. Like he was looking for something.'

'Is Benjamin back?'

Riley shook his head.

Marcus rubbed the sleep out of his eyes and sat up. 'Creepy git. Probably nicking Benjamin's things after getting rid of him.'

Riley's bottom lip trembled. 'Do you think Motley killed Benjamin?'

Marcus shook his head reassuringly. 'No.' Then he shrugged, 'I don't know. He must have something to do with it. Benjamin wouldn't just leave without telling me.'

'And me.' Riley sniffed and wiped his nose on his sleeve.

Marcus smiled and messed up Riley's hair. 'Yeah. And you.'

The boys' attention turned to a soft thud from downstairs. Riley looked at Marcus. 'Hester's home,' he said in a low voice.

Marcus shook his head and pointed to the window. 'Nah, I watched her stumble up to the house a few hours ago. She was so drunk she could hardly walk. We won't see her until tomorrow tea time.'

Marcus got out of bed quietly and crept to the door to peer down the corridor. 'Where's Motley?' he mouthed the words to Riley.

'He left and I heard him go downstairs. That's when I came and got you.'

'C'mon.' Marcus waved Riley over to him. They crept slowly along the corridor and down the stairs. As they approached the last step, they could hear Motley chanting in a low voice.

Marcus turned to Riley. 'He's singing something.'

Riley nodded. 'What?' he mouthed.

Marcus shrugged.

Riley hugged Marcus' leg as they carefully peered out from the stairs. Motley stood a few feet in front of the cellar door, chanting something in another language. In his hands he held a pewter cross. Coiled around the cross was a pewter snake, its neck and head wrapped tightly around the top. It moved slowly, clenching itself tighter around the cross. Motley held it high above his head and chanted slightly louder, this time in English. Marcus listened closely and was able to pick up the last few words.

...may darkness now choke the breath out of light.

Motley lowered his hands and walked towards the cellar door. He hit it with the same soft thud Marcus and Riley heard earlier and was bounced back.

'Mental.' Marcus mouthed to Riley who nodded.

They looked back to Motley whose eyes were closed. Before they could blink, Motley dissolved into grains of black sand and fell to the floor. The patch of sand moved towards the crack at the bottom of the cellar door. It too was bounced back, this time with a flash of light.

The patch lingered for a moment and then moved across the floor and up the wall, dissolving into it.

The house became deathly quiet. Then Marcus heard the faint sound of trickling water beside him. His feet were warm and wet. He looked down at Riley whose face had turned white and his eyes were fixed on the far wall.

'Let's get you cleaned up,' Marcus said to Riley. 'And then you can bunk with me.'

5

Gideon

The air had changed. Benjamin forced his eyes open, unsettled by the picture he had just seen. Mist sprayed his face gently and he heard the sounds of rushing water in the distance.

Primrose lay down and Jeems helped Benjamin off her back. Benjamin could only guess how far she had taken them from the furls. The edge of the forest was behind them, and directly in front was a wide river, flowing for as far as he could see. Without trees to block it, the sun shone down and burned through the watery spray. Across the river in the distance was a thick blanket of fog that covered a huge space of land. Circular in shape, it hung low and heavy over the ground, like a blanket. The gentle breeze did nothing to move it along.

'C'mon, this way, before we're seen.' Benjamin jumped at Jeems' voice. Glancing over his shoulder, he saw a huge waterfall that cascaded over the centre of some cliffs and plunged into the river below.

'Where are we going?' He asked timidly, following Jeems in the direction of the waterfall.

'We'll have ter get ter Gideon this way,' sputtered Jeems through a forced cough. Benjamin noticed Jeems was limping and looked down to find a nasty gash on his left ankle.

'You're bleeding! Can you – '

'Can't really talk right now, if ya don't mind,' said Jeems through clenched teeth. He struggled to keep his balance. Primrose came up alongside and supported him gently with her nose.

'Sorry,' responded Benjamin. 'I bet it hurts. It's just so weird here, and I have so many questions.'

'Questions that need answers. And answers you will get - in time.'

Benjamin nearly jumped out of his skin when it seemed out of nowhere appeared a tall man. With shoulder length greying brown hair swept back from his face and a beard down to his waist, he was the strangest looking man Benjamin had ever seen. His long light grey robes hung loosely over his slender body. However strange he looked, Benjamin felt oddly comforted by this man's presence, as though he had known him forever.

'Hello, Benjamin,' said the man.

Benjamin was stunned. 'How did you know my name?'

'Is that not the name you have been known by?' The stranger's eyes searched Benjamin's face intently. 'You have grown. You look just like - . Well, that can wait. My name is Gideon, and here just in time, I would say.'

'Some help here would be grand,' said Jeems breathlessly.

The man strode over to Jeems. He patted Primrose and then bent down to inspect Jeems' injured leg. 'My dear Jeems, this is a problem. We have no time to lose. Quickly, Benjamin, grasp my cloak.' Without wanting to ask any questions, Benjamin grabbed a handful of the soft grey robe. Cradling Jeems under his arm, the man named Gideon raised his staff up in the air and muttered something that Benjamin couldn't understand.

Benjamin felt his body disintegrate into a million fragments and then come back together again. He blinked his eyes and checked that he was still in one piece.

'What – How? Benjamin looked around. 'I'm not by the river anymore, am I?' He asked nobody. He looked around briefly and then realised where he was. 'We're on the other side of the waterfall!'

'Welcome to my humble abode, Benjamin,' replied Gideon. 'I call it Water's Hyde.'

The pounding drone of the waterfall behind him, Benjamin stood still while his eyes adjusted to the dim light. Soft flames from the torches along the rock walls glowed warmly. It wasn't until Gideon caught Benjamin's eye that he realised the man was trying to talk to him.

'What? … I can't hear you.' Benjamin shook his head and pointed to the waterfall that had swallowed Gideon's voice.

With a wave of Gideon's hand the sound of the falling water was silenced.

'There. Finally,' sighed the greying man, looking proudly at the hushed waterfall. 'Beautiful and useful, but most distracting at times. And sometimes not at all helpful when speaking to guests.' Gideon peered at Benjamin intermittently over the glasses he just put on while he took bottles of various liquids from the large wooden table and piled them into his arms. 'Oh dear, my eyesight is not what it used to be.' Gideon edged under a floating torch to read one of the labels. The light blue flames seemed to shine brighter as Gideon moved beneath them, as if they were under his command. Now that he had more light, Benjamin looked around in amazement.

He was standing in a large open cave with dry rock walls. To his left was a stone hearth with blue and green flames blazing in it. The kettle that was hissing and steaming above the fire floated in mid-air. A large portrait of the landscape hung above the hearth. Squinting hard, he saw slight movements in the portrait. In the middle of the mantle was a suspended set of scales surrounded by blue rays of light that interconnected and formed a ball around it. One end of the scale was slightly higher than the other, and in the middle was a round medallion a little larger than a one pound coin.

The room was lined with shelves that were filled with dusty bottles of various things, trinkets and jars of bits and pieces. There were jars of dried crickets, dragonfly wings, dead dandelions, and much more Benjamin couldn't identify. In one corner was a pile of old cauldrons, some with holes in the bottom.

Towards the back, Benjamin noticed three archways that led down different corridors. The blue torches overhead cast a soft glow as he approached them. Losing his nerve, he decided to retreat to where Gideon was tending to Jeems.

'Are you a doctor?' Benjamin asked Gideon as he watched him pour assorted liquids into a shiny cup.

'I have been known to restore the odd one or two to health,' the old man said, never taking his eyes off of what he was doing. Benjamin watched him intently for a moment, finding it hard to hold back all the questions he had.

'How did we get here from the river? And how did you know my name?'

Gideon smiled. 'You are every bit as curious as I had hoped you'd be,' he replied. He gave Jeems a drink and rose from his bedside. 'I shimmered us here from the river to help Jeems avoid a most dreadful future. His actions, although heroic, ended in a way I had not anticipated. And so the plans that were made have had to be altered, but only slightly, I hope.' He strolled over to the moving portrait above the fireplace and studied it for a few moments before he spoke again. 'I will need to keep a watchful eye on him, but I do think that you deserve answers to some of your questions.'

Gideon gestured towards two chairs that were tucked under the big wooden table. They scraped along the cold stone floor as he drew them out.

'You asked how I knew your name. The answer to that is simply this – I knew your name because I have always known it. Meridia is your home. It is no accident that you are here. I sent for you when the time was right.'

'What?' Benjamin asked, dumbstruck.

Gideon smiled. 'Your dream of last night was no accident, Benjamin.'

Benjamin sat in silence for a moment. '… those stars and the message on the door,' he trailed off.

Gideon nodded. 'They are full of zing.' He leaned into Benjamin, 'they were most excited to have finally found you.'

Benjamin tried to pick one question from the hundreds in his head.

'You said Meridia was my home – am I going to live here now?' He squeezed the arms of the chair, trying not to let his excitement show.

'Ah. Now that is a very good question. And naturally with all good questions comes very long answers. I'm afraid, Benjamin, that for me to answer you properly would take more time than we have tonight. I am mindful that after everything you have gone through, what you need most is a good night's rest.'

It wasn't until Gideon mentioned sleep that Benjamin realised how tired he was.

He yawned. 'I'm not sure I'll be able to sleep.'

Gideon chuckled and stood up. 'Water's Hyde has an amazing way of leading sleep to those who need it.' Gideon gestured towards Jeems who was lying on a bed a few feet away, shivering and drenched in sweat. 'It will take a few days to make sure that Jeems does not meet an untimely fate and turn into a furl, so we will have plenty of time for questions.'

Too tired to argue, Benjamin followed Gideon to the back of the cave and turned right into one of the dark corridors he had seen earlier. As he entered a room, dim lights along the walls revealed a simply made bed and bedside table. On the table was a mug with steam rising out of it and three chocolate biscuits on a plate.

'Something for comfort,' Gideon said gently and ushered Benjamin through. 'I always feel better after a cup of hot chocolate and a few biscuits. You should find everything you need in the wardrobe. Good night, Benjamin.'

'Night.' Before Benjamin could turn to say anything else, Gideon was gone. The wardrobe was full of clothes just his size, and in no time he had found a set of pyjamas and was in bed with his plate of biscuits beside him and his drink in his hands.

Benjamin looked around, surprised at how dry and warm the walls were despite the fact that he was in the middle of a mountain behind a waterfall. Gideon had called the walls a homely touch. Benjamin drank his drink and smiled at the thought of living here forever.

He wiped the inside of his cup clean with his finger. The only drink Hester ever gave them was water. With the last crunch of his biscuit, Benjamin's eyes grew heavy and he drifted off to sleep.

6

The Oracle

Benjamin rubbed his nose. And again. Something tickled his face. Without opening his eyes, Benjamin yawned lazily and made a motion to shoo it away. After a third time, Benjamin opened one eye and was met with two little black beady ones, a cold, wet, quivering nose and very long whiskers.

'Ah!' Benjamin scrambled to a sitting position in his bed. The little furry creature made a loud ticking noise and scurried away.

Benjamin got out of bed and followed the little creature into the main room where he found Gideon talking to it.

'Yes, it is him,' said the old man lovingly, nose to nose with the little brown animal that had perched itself on the table. Benjamin watched its long body, short legs and furry tail twitch and jump.

'*Tch tcchhh ttcchh tch tch tch.*'

'No, I don't think he has brought you any chocolate buttons,' Gideon replied. 'How could he have possibly known your fondness for them?' Gideon cradled the animal in his arms before he looked up and noticed Benjamin standing there. 'Ah, good morning Benjamin. Please forgive Greyfriars, he was hoping for some chocolate. Quite hooked on it, I'm afraid. I suppose I have only myself to blame. How was your sleep?' Gideon scrunched up his nose to hold his glasses in place as Greyfriars climbed to the top of Gideon's hat. Gideon raised his top lip and showed a set of very crooked teeth from behind his thick moustache and beard.

'Cup of tea?' Gideon asked, a steaming kettle in his hand.

'Er – yes please.' Benjamin sat down at a small rectangular wooden table with two benches on either side that he had not noticed the night before. The entire room was much brighter than the previous night. Benjamin looked up and noticed the cave just kept going up without a ceiling to stop it.

Gideon noticed Benjamin's puzzled look and raised his head. 'I use it to help me remember when to wake up. I do like a lie-in. I daresay I would sleep myself into an early grave if given the chance.' Gideon chuckled to himself and passed a cup of milky tea to Benjamin. Benjamin gripped the cup with both hands and gazed down into it. He could feel Gideon watching him and was a bit relieved when he finally heard him ask, 'I trust you still have questions?'

'Yeah.' Benjamin's eyes never left his cup of tea. From the other side of the hearth Jeems moaned. 'How's Jeems?'

'He's pulled through the night well. He's strong and has a good spirit. I should think he will be fine by tomorrow.'

'Does that mean I'll be staying here until at least tomorrow?' Benjamin asked, trying to hide his enthusiasm. 'I mean, it's fine by me, but I think even Hester will be wondering where I am.'

'I should think your stay with us will extend beyond tomorrow,' responded Gideon. He smiled as Benjamin shifted with excitement. 'And don't worry about Hester.'

Benjamin gulped his tea down, his mind preoccupied with what Gideon was capable of doing to Hester the Horrible. From what he had seen of Gideon already he was sure Hester would be turned into a toad or something equally disgusting.

Gideon shuffled over to a large pan suspended above the fire. 'I think we should have a spot of breakfast.'

Breakfast was a grand affair, or it was for Benjamin. A full fry-up was something he had only ever seen on Hester's plate on a Sunday morning. The thought of her faded from his mind as his breakfast warmed his belly.

'Shall we move to the warmth of the fire?' Gideon motioned towards the large hearth. Before Benjamin could ask where they were going to sit, he saw two lovely brown suede armchairs appear before his eyes in front of the hearth. 'After you,' said Gideon with a twinkle in his eyes. He smiled at Benjamin's astounded expression. Benjamin sank into the soft brown chair while Gideon tended to Jeems before coming to sit across from him.

Gideon cleared his throat. 'Furls are evil tricksters who draw blood from anyone who tries to pass through them. You have now seen what they are capable of. They are in Meridia for two reasons. The first is to warn their master of any visitors to Meridia. The second is to turn whoever they bite into one of them. Although one more day is needed, I am certain that Jeems has escaped such an undesirable fate.'

'Jeems was almost turned into a furl? And who's their master? He doesn't sound like anybody I'd want to meet.'

'For the moment, we are talking about a *she*,' explained Gideon patiently. 'Magh is her name. Her followers call her Queen Magh. She rules over no lands at present. However, she has, sadly, been responsible for the devastation of many. Her goal is to have ultimate power over not only Meridia, but the rest of the world, including where you have been living.'

'So if she doesn't rule over anything then how come she has followers?' Benjamin asked.

'To get into the detail of it is too horrible even for me. But simply, she was created for one purpose - to trick people into thinking she can give them what they want. By tricking and lying she has created a group of followers, destroying both them and a large part of Meridia at the same time. The furls are merely one of the many ways in which she has led those like you into a life of hurt and sadness.'

'So there are more people in Meridia?' Benjamin asked.

Gideon sighed heavily and gazed at the moving portrait. 'There was a time when Meridia was full of the bustle and laughter of people. One by one Magh sought people out who were lost and lonely and tricked them into following her, and it has meant their doom. She has been given powers that wreak havoc, chaos and disaster.'

'Someone created her to be like that?'

'Yes, but one day, she will realise that she has been deceived the same way as the ones before her. Her creator will never let her have ultimate power.' Gideon put his hand up to Benjamin who opened his mouth. 'That story is very long and best left for another time.'

'She sounds terrible.'

Gideon nodded. 'At the height of her power she was able to command some of Meridia. But she made a mistake and was sent into hiding.'

'What happened?' Benjamin moved to the edge of his seat.

'Her greed clouded her judgement. But what matters now is that she is slowly beginning to get stronger, and the last thing we want is for Magh to begin her destructive rampage once again.' Gideon stared intently into the fire, stroking Greyfriars who had climbed down from his hat and curled into his lap. 'And that, my dear boy, is where you come in.'

Benjamin looked at Gideon in astonishment. 'What? What do I have to do with any of it?'

'I believe you to be the one to stop Magh.'

'But why would you pick me? I'm nobody. I'm just –
me.' Benjamin forced the words out.

Gideon looked up at Benjamin over his glasses.
'Because you are just you. And would it make you feel any
better if I told you I didn't pick you, Benjamin. You were
always meant to save Meridia from the forces of Magh.'

Benjamin looked blankly at the old man.

Gideon was thoughtful. 'Hmm. Let me see if I can't be
clearer. You live in a children's home, is that right?'

'Yes,' Benjamin responded, unable to hide the surprise
in his voice.

'Hadley Priest?' Gideon continued.

'How did you know that?'

'Magh is not the only one around here with a trick or
two up her sleeve,' said Gideon. 'Tell me, Benjamin, what do
you know about your parents?'

Benjamin shrugged. 'Nothing, really. I've lived at the
home ever since I can remember. Whenever I've asked Hester
she's always said I was found there.'

Gideon sat thoughtfully for a moment. 'Hester is right,
to some extent. You see, Benjamin, Meridia is your home. I
called you back when the time was right. And, although you
have not been cared for as I would have hoped, you are here
nonetheless.' Gideon looked fondly at Benjamin. 'My dear

boy, what a story you have yet to be told. Both your mother and father would have been very, very proud.'

Benjamin's eyes widened and his throat constricted. Eventually he managed to utter, 'you, you, know my parents?' It was almost unbelievable, how this funny looking man could have known the two people Benjamin most wanted to meet. 'Where are they? What's happened to them?'

'I *knew* your parents well, Benjamin. They were very loyal and trustworthy people.' Gideon's eyes didn't leave Benjamin's. 'The look on your face tells me you already know what I'm about to say.'

Benjamin's mouth went dry. He could feel a heavy weight in the pit of his stomach. Gideon said he *knew* his parents. That could only mean one thing. Benjamin tried to swallow despite his bone dry mouth and throat. He could feel his eyes welling up with tears. There was a ringing in his ears and his head began to throb. He always knew deep down that his parents would never have just left him at Hadley Priest. He knew there was an explanation.

Looking up into Gideon's kindly face, Benjamin gathered up the courage to ask the question he knew he didn't want the answer to. 'Are you saying that my parents are, are, *gone?*' Tears dripped from his cheek as he closed his eyes and bowed his head.

Gideon was silent for a moment. When he did speak, his words pierced Benjamin like a hot knife. 'Both of your parents died at the hands of Magh, during her days of causing chaos and destruction to gain power. As I said previously, there is no limit to what Magh will do. To her, power over everything is what she was destined for.'

Benjamin couldn't speak. His shoulders heaved with sobs he initially tried to silence, but Gideon's hand on his back was enough to let go and the pain of ten years spilled out.

At last, Benjamin dried his eyes and looked up into Gideon's face, now only inches away. 'So my parents were tricked by Magh, like some of the others you were talking about?'

'Your parents remained good to the end. The entire story of how they fell will unfold as you continue on in Meridia, but they stayed true to their hearts. That is the very thing that sent Magh into a rage, and eventually caused her downfall.'

'So why am I so special?'

Gideon looked around Water's Hyde before giving an answer. 'Benjamin, do you remember when you confronted Hester on the stairs?'

Benjamin nodded. 'I don't think I'll ever forget that.'

'Have you ever felt able to do that before? Stand up to someone you thought was doing something wrong?'

Benjamin thought for a moment. He had always been a bit of a chicken when it came to standing up to anyone. 'No,' he said glumly.

'What was it, do you think, that allowed you to do it that night? That night when Hester was treating little Riley so badly?'

'I don't know.' Benjamin shrugged. 'I can't explain it, it just – happened.'

Gideon nodded. 'I suppose then, you wouldn't be able to explain how you managed to turn the stairs into a slide?'

Benjamin's eyes widened in amazement. 'So I *did* do it!' He shook his head. 'No, I definitely can't explain how I did that!'

'Well, I have an idea as to how you were able to do it, so that is why I sent for you.'

'I'm sorry, I don't understand.' Benjamin looked at Gideon, more confused than ever.

Gideon stood up and Greyfriars landed on all fours. He moved in front of the hearth to look at the portrait of the moving landscape.

'Many years ago an oracle was spoken in Meridia. It spoke of the 'one intended', the only person who was able to save both the land and the people.'

'So how does that involve me?' Benjamin shifted uncomfortably in his chair.

'Some of it is still unclear, but it refers to a child who has a pure heart.' Gideon turned to look at Benjamin. 'I'm convinced that the child it talks about is you.'

It took a moment before Benjamin was able to reply. He eventually got out the words. 'How do you know for sure?'

Gideon sighed. 'It would mean travelling to the Bogwump people. They protect the oracle. Once an oracle is spoken, it is laid to rest in the bog. The only person who can raise it out of the bog is the one it speaks of.'

'So, say I go to the Bogwump people, and I get the oracle. Then you will know that I'm the one that's supposed to fight Magh.'

'Precisely.'

Benjamin sat in silence for a while, dizzy with all the things he had heard. He really didn't want to be back at Hadley Priest. And he wanted to get back at Magh for taking his parents away from him. But fighting her? That sounded dangerous. 'But what if I have to fight Magh? I mean, how?' She has powers, and I – well, I'll never have that kind of power.' He asked Gideon as he rubbed his hands on the arms of the chair and looked down.

Gideon leaned towards Benjamin. 'Do not underestimate yourself. If, as I suspect, you are the one intended for this journey, you will do things you never thought possible. And let me assure you that a battle between you and Magh is not about to happen any time soon. And *if* it should happen in the future, you will not be alone.'

'You'll be with me?' Benjamin asked solemnly.

'Every step of the way.'

Benjamin thought about his parents and felt a surge of anger towards Magh. 'Okay,' he said and stood up. 'Let's go.'

7

Water's Hyde

Gideon wasted no time and quickly started to pull out old maps and parchments with writing on it. As soon as Jeems was feeling better they began to pack and plan the trip to the Bogwumps. Although Benjamin was very curious about it all, it was hardly anything he could sink his teeth into. He had no idea what any of the parchments said, and the maps were of places he had never heard of before.

'What's a *Bear's Nook?*' Benjamin asked when trying to make sense of an old map of Meridia. Of all the questions he had been asking over the past few days, none got Gideon's attention more than that one. He quickly came over to Benjamin's side of the table and looked at the map in front of him.

'*Brae's Nook*,' Gideon corrected Benjamin, 'is a village where people once lived.' 'Just like all the other ones that you see along the river and into the fields, Magh destroyed them all.' Gideon followed the map along the river with his finger and Benjamin guessed he was lost in a memory.

Jeems came out from one of the back rooms, loaded down with pots, sleeping mats and food. 'A little help here,' he grunted. By the time Benjamin noticed him, Jeems lost his footing and went crashing down with his load tumbling down around him.

Benjamin raced over to help Jeems collect the stray items. As he did so, something caught his eye. Crawling under the table to get a closer look, Benjamin realised it was an old key. It looked as though it had once been shiny, but the bronze had tarnished and had turned green in some places.

'What door does this key open?' Benjamin asked, climbing out from under the table. He stood up and let the key dangle from its silver string.

'Ah. Thank you, Benjamin. It must have dislodged itself when Jeems tripped. I will take it.' Gideon approached Benjamin quickly, and motioned with his hand for Benjamin to give it to him. Benjamin hesitated at first, looking at it. Gideon's hand closed around it and gently prised it out of Benjamin's hand. Gazing kindly at him, Gideon put it in a pocket inside of his cloak and turned away.

Although Benjamin was getting restless, he couldn't say he was bored at Water's Hyde. He had spent most of his time exploring the cave and everything in it. Gideon had given more homely touches to Water's Hyde than Benjamin had originally realised, and it wasn't long before he found a very large back garden, complete with a fish pond and a huge oak tree that he would sit in for hours. It was also the home of Hagar, a beautiful white winged horse. Three times the size of a normal horse, with long flowing hair so white it looked like a silver robe. Hagar was by far the most beautiful creature Benjamin had ever seen. Every day Benjamin went to the garden and sat in the oak tree. Hagar would come out of the trees and stop just along the border of the garden.

'I am keeping her for a friend of mine,' Gideon told Benjamin one day after he asked about Hagar.

'Who?'

'A friend that will one day be your friend, too,' Gideon had said.

When Benjamin wasn't in the garden, he was examining all the trinkets Gideon had jammed in wall units and shelves that lined the main room of Water's Hyde.

Everything from medals to toothbrushes was in the rows upon rows of shelves and cabinets. Most of the things Benjamin picked up were very odd looking, but there were some that looked like normal, everyday things, except they weren't. Benjamin especially liked the small animal figurines that came to life when he touched them. He enjoyed playing with these until he was bitten by a mother polar bear. Glass tumblers that grew legs jumped down from the shelves and ran around the room until they either smashed to bits or were chased back up by Greyfriars. What looked like an innocent pair of cufflinks turned into handcuffs, binding Benjamin until Gideon could remember how to unbind them. The most dazzling item of all, Benjamin decided, was the hand carved wand he found in a tarnished silver box.

'Is this a wizard's wand?' Benjamin asked, looking at the wooden stick with great interest. It was a goldish colour and slightly crooked near the base. When Benjamin took it out, he noticed a bright green leaf near the tip. Gideon looked at the wand reproachfully. He closed the box gently before he took it away from Benjamin.

'This came from the highest branch of the largest Golden Yew tree in Meridia,' Gideon said, and his eyes flashed back to another time.

Benjamin broke the silence. 'So you *are* a wizard. I thought so. I mean, there was no other explanation. All these magical things - the ceiling, the waterfall.'

Gideon sighed and turned his gaze to Benjamin. After some time he answered. 'I could see how you might think that. But this wand is not, nor ever was, mine. I am... I am what I am.'

Benjamin had no idea what Gideon meant. When he plucked up the courage to ask, Gideon turned his back and disappeared with the wand through one of the doors in the corridor. He came back empty-handed. Benjamin thought it unwise to question him anymore.

Since being at Water's Hyde, Benjamin dreamed about Hadley Priest and the others. Not that he missed it. On the contrary, he was quite happy where he was. His dreams were everyday things that would normally happen at Hadley Priest. Once he dreamed that Riley was walking around with a pot on his head and a wooden spoon in his hand shouting, 'Death to tyrants!' He was going around the whole house squishing ants and spiders until Hester finally caught up with him. She grabbed the wooden spoon out of his hand and smacked it against the side of the pot that was on his head. Once Riley got his hearing back she sent him to bed. Benjamin thought these dreams a good deal better than the one he had been having before he left Hadley Priest, and definitely better than what he saw the day he closed his eyes on the back of Primrose, so didn't give them much thought.

Days went by before Gideon finally announced they would be leaving in the morning. Benjamin and Jeems were in the garden making airplanes out of paper and watching them fly through the air.

'Hey, Gideon, look,' said Benjamin. 'All you have to do is fold the paper into an airplane, and it goes all by itself. Duck!'

Gideon managed to dodge a red double-prop plane as it whizzed by his glasses. 'Yes, I do seem to recall how much fun I had with pollywinder paper when I was a boy.' Gideon smiled as he watched two jets go in for a landing.

Gideon turned his attention away from the planes and focused on Benjamin. 'Have you enjoyed your stay, Benjamin?'

'Oh yes, loads,' answered Benjamin immediately.

As a fighter jet struggled to get out of his beard and fly away, Gideon continued, 'Good, but the time has come for you to move on. That is why everything is ready for you to set out in the morning.'

The words hit Benjamin hard. Although he had expected it, somehow Benjamin felt anxious. 'Me? Me?' He managed to utter. 'I thought we were going together?' Panic choked Benjamin's voice and his stomach flipped.

Gideon advanced on him slowly. 'You are not going by yourself. You will of course be going with Jeems and Primrose. Jeems knows Meridia as well as I do and I trust him with my life. He knows what he must do.'

'But you said you would come with me.'

Gideon looked down at Benjamin and smiled. 'Just because I will not be walking beside you where you can see me doesn't mean I won't be with you. I was able to see you at Hadley Priest, wasn't I?'

Benjamin dug the toe of his shoe into the ground. 'I still haven't been able to figure that one out,' he mumbled.

There was a long silence. Gideon had made the sky dark and the stars twinkled above. Benjamin swung on the tyre swing that hung from the huge oak tree. Hagar, who was normally content to watch from the trees that surrounded the garden, came out from her protective shelter and raised her head to Benjamin as if to encourage him. He thought back to the night he had snuck in to the garden and had seen Gideon talking to Hagar. It seemed that Hagar understood Gideon.

Benjamin swung silently, looking at Gideon, full of confusion and anxiety.

'So we are going to the Bogwumps? Is that right?' he asked. He shifted his eyes between Gideon and Jeems, who was trying without success to brush Primrose's teeth.

Gideon spoke first. 'Yes, that is correct. As you know, the Bogwumps possess the gift of foresight. It is a gift that was bestowed upon them many, many years ago. Some think that foresight is a power, rather than a gift, and many have sought the Bogwumps out to steal it, so they are well guarded by the bog that they live in. Once you raise the oracle, as I am sure you will, the next part of your journey will begin.'

Benjamin opened his mouth to speak but Gideon held his hand up. 'I think it best not to think about the next part until you get to the Bogwumps. You would do well to be in their company for a while.'

Jeems' voice came from behind them. 'Fine! Get a toothache! But don't yer think fer one second that I'm gonna be stoppin' ter find yer any root of elicampe when yer can't eat fer the pain!' Jeems threw a very large toothbrush down in frustration.

Primrose gave a smoky *humph* and settled down for the night.

'We should be headin' ter bed. We got a long way ter go termorrow, so we do.' Jeems mumbled, glaring at Primrose.

Thoughts plagued Benjamin's mind as he tried to go to sleep. What exactly would he have to do when he got to the Bogwumps? And what if he wasn't the one that Gideon thought he was? Would they send him back? As Benjamin's eyes got heavier and he went to sleep, he found himself in another dream.

He dreamed he was back at Hadley Priest. ...Riley was scooping ants into a jar ... Marcus was next to Riley putting the ants into Hester's socks. ... All three of them were laughing...Benjamin turned to Hester behind them. ... Benjamin ran...

....Benjamin ran onto a field... in front of him was a giant tree that reached up to the sky. ...animals of every kind were in the tree.... nesting in it....eating from it...under the tree were people....children were playing....Benjamin looked over to a woman with a sad face....he walked over to her... she looked past him and let out a scream...

.... He turned around to a huge swarm of black flies heading toward the tree... they were in the shape of a tornado... they covered the tree and destroyed it... the leaves were gone and the tree was dead.... The swarm turned on the people and animals....it devoured all of them.... It turned to Benjamin and swarmed around him....suddenly he was standing on a rock ..... the swarm tried to lift him from the rock he was standing on but couldn't...Benjamin felt it try to suffocate him ... he could hear the screams of all the people but he couldn't see them....they were in the swarm....they were pleading for their lives....

Benjamin woke suddenly, his hands over his ears. He blinked twice and noticed a flicker of light on the corridor wall outside his room. The stone floor felt surprisingly warm on his bare feet as he got out of bed and followed the short tunnel out into the main area. The fire in the front room flickered in the hearth, dancing to Gideons' finger that was tapping on his mug. Jeems snored loudly from the far corner. Quietly, Benjamin approached Gideon.

'Oh, I'm sorry. Did my thinking wake you? I do sometimes tend to do it out loud.' Gideon motioned for Benjamin to stand in front of him.

Benjamin shook his head. 'I had a dream,' he replied, rubbing the sleep out of his eyes. Gideon stroked Greyfriars and paused before responding.

'Would I be right in thinking you dream often? Both day and night?' Gideon put Greyfriars down. Benjamin watched as the little animal stumbled over to the rug in front of the fire and collapsed on it with a sleepy heaviness.

'Sometimes.' Benjamin looked up to the scales that hung suspended on the mantle. 'I used to have the same dream over and over again until I came here. Now most of them are about Hadley Priest, but some of them are scary. And when we were running from the furls something strange happened when I closed my eyes. It wasn't a dream because I wasn't asleep, but it was like I could see a movie in my mind.'

Gideon motioned for Benjamin to sit down. 'Do take care in your dreams. I would think that they are best kept to yourself for the time being.'

Benjamin sighed deeply. 'What are those?' he asked, pointing to the scales on the mantle. They teetered just out of balance with one another.

Gideon got up to fetch them, turning his back on Benjamin. He turned back with the scales slightly suspended over his cupped hands. 'These scales represent the balance between good and evil. One side is the good in Meridia, and the other is Magh and the people in her service. As you can see right now, they are relatively even but they were not always like this. Lately Magh's side has gotten heavier, bringing the other side in almost equal to hers. This means that even as we speak Magh is getting stronger. The only way to see good defeat Magh is to secure the four leagues that have been scattered throughout Meridia.'

'What are leagues?' Benjamin asked. 'I haven't heard anything about them before.'

'You will hear more about them when you raise the oracle.' Gideon turned back and replaced the scales on the mantle, looking worried.

Gideon continued, 'the journey you are about to go on is long. The way is difficult. You may very well meet up with those who would want to see you fail. Some challenges will be more difficult than others. You may need to fight for your life.'

Benjamin's mouth felt dry. Gideon smiled reassuringly before going on, 'So, I thought I would give you a few things to help you along the way.' As he sat back down he drew a small bundle of rope from under his cloak.

'This rope will never break unless you need it to. It will be as long or as short as you need it to be.' Gideon handed the soft, white bundle to Benjamin. 'It will change to any colour and even turn invisible.' Benjamin examined the thin rope. It looked too fragile to be unbreakable, and he hoped he would never have to find out.

'This staff,' Gideon said, twisting around to get a beautifully carved staff from behind the chair, 'was made by me from the Vie tree. The branch was freely given to me by the tree to make this staff, and as a result it has some very special properties. Like your rope, this, too, will not break. It is very strong and when used, will give a blow with the same strength as a thousand men.'

Benjamin took it in his hand, amazed at how light it was. The staff looked thicker and longer when Gideon had it, but fitted Benjamin perfectly. Gideon went back to the mantle and fetched something from it.

'The last thing I am going to give you is this.' The medallion from the middle of the scales dangled on a gold chain in front of Benjamin. 'This is the Arcrux. You won't need until the next part of your journey, but I thought you should have it now.'

'Hey, I've seen that before. I have it around my neck in the dream I'd always have at Hadley Priest.' Benjamin studied the medallion before putting it around his neck. It was as thick as a one pound coin and was divided into four parts. The front had a door to each chamber with the letters E, W, F, W on them.

Gideon nodded. 'I think you will find your dreams to be very helpful to you, and others, in the future. But for now, if there is one piece of advice that I will give you that will be more valuable than all the rest it is this - keep the Arcrux hidden from view. Although I am not convinced Magh would be able to touch it now, she would do anything to get her hands on it.'

Following an awkward silence, Gideon looked into Benjamin's eyes. 'I sometimes wondered if this day would ever come. Meridia has had no hope for so many years, and now it looks like hope is renewed.'

Benjamin held the staff next to him. 'But you said we don't know for sure if I'm even the one that should be here. What happens if I'm not?'

'I wouldn't let that worry you, I am not wrong often.' Gideon responded, winking. 'Right,' Gideon straightened up and rubbed his hands together. 'You must get back to bed.'

Benjamin lay awake, one hand wrapped around his staff and the other around the Arcrux. What Gideon said had frightened him. Fighting for his life? How was he going to do this? He was just a boy, and who exactly was he supposed to be fighting? Magh? The one who made her? It was all so much to take in. He tried to think of better thoughts and his mind drifted to the dream he had about Riley and Marcus putting ants in Hester's socks.

'If only,' he said and closed his eyes.

8

The Face in the Fire

Outside Water's Hyde, the spray from the waterfall danced over the bubbling river. On the other side of the river the sun rose in the distance, its light filtering down on Meridia south of the blanket of fog. A raven was perched on a rock between Water's Hyde and the heavy patch of fog. Barely noticeable in the dawn, it made a cawing sound, its beak clamped tightly around a torn piece of blue cloth. The raven looked in a fore bidding manner at the fog before it turned towards the waterfall. A new day in Meridia had dawned, and the raven had something to deliver.

With one huge flap of its wings, the raven rose above the morning clouds and flew northwards. Within hours it was flying over lands where the sun was not known and the grass was dry and barren. The once open green spaces had been consumed by black trees, twisted and jagged, devoid of leaves and with thorns piercing out of them. The raven descended and flew confidently through the tangled growth, gliding and turning without ruffling a feather. It picked up speed and headed into a knotted mass of trees at the northernmost tip of Meridia.

The raven's wind touched one of the sharp thorns and vanished into thin air witha popping sound. Its only remains being a few small feathers that floated serenely to the ground.

'My lady, the scout has returned.' Another huge black raven hopped to the foot of a black iron chair. Its head was cocked upwards, and it spoke to the figure who sat in the huge throne.

'Send him in. I'm most anxious to hear of any news.'

The raven from the river glided into the hall where the woman sat. It dodged rocks that both hung down from the low ceiling and jutted out from the craggy ground. The hall was dimly lit with red torches and fires that stained the rough walls bright red and orange. Other ravens settled high up in crevices amongst the dirt walls, their huge yellow eyes gleaming in the firelight. To the right of the woman's throne was a small gathering of beasts. Somewhat human in form but with beastly faces, they grunted and howled like animals, fighting over scraps of food the woman had thrown at them.

The raven came before the woman, and gave a slight bow before it perched itself on the arm of the chair. The blue cloth still dangled from its beak.

The woman reached out her hand and the raven dropped the cloth into it. 'Well Drach, what have you found?' She asked the raven in a smooth, deep voice.

The woman held the bit of cloth up to her nose. 'Ah, I see my furls have been busy,' she said with a smile, sliding her

69

long thin finger over the drops of blood that had stained the blue fabric. 'Let's see who this belongs to.' Closing her deep black eyes, she sniffed the piece of cloth.

The woman opened her eyes, gingerly fingering the cloth. A sly smile slid across her face. 'Tsk, tsk, Gideon. What a naughty old fool you have been to try and keep this from me.' She turned to the raven she called Drach. 'The child has come back, and not a moment too soon. He will be on his way into the fog. You must follow him there.'

Drach squawked and, with a single flap of his wings rose and was out of sight. Her long thin face grimaced as she sniffed the cloth again.

'Strange,' she said to herself. 'There is another here. It's not that old fool Gideon, foul smelling creature that he is.' She skewed up her face as she walked towards a huge fire. 'And yet, it is definitely not the boy.' She stared at the fire thoughtfully. 'Who would have been foolish enough to pull him out of my furls?' She threw the cloth into the fire and spoke out in a clear strong voice.

Unknown to me now, but soon not to be; show me the face who set the child free

The fire roared ferociously and spat out across the floor. In the flames the shape of a man-like figure appeared, showing a droopy, long face and uneven hair. The woman's eyes widened and she laughed.

70

'It can't be!' She turned from the fire and strode back to her chair. 'Gideon I do give you too much credit,' she said. 'I don't know how you found him, but you will be eternally sorry you did.' She turned her head upwards and addressed the audience of ravens. 'My darlings, have you seen? Have you seen who the old man has found?' A great sea of cawing rose in the hall. The woman put up her hands and the ravens silenced immediately. 'Yes, yes. I thought we had taken care of him. But somehow he is leading the child to the oracle. We can't have that now, can we?' She circled the fire. 'This child will meet the same fate as his parents,' she said to herself in a cold voice before approaching the group of creatures that were huddled to one side.

'Queen Magh will not be made a fool of. It is time to take care of this once and for all!' She advanced towards the creature, full of anger. She picked up one of the creatures and threw him into the fire. The squeals of pain coming from the fire could scarcely be heard over the cawing and squawking of the ravens overhead. The fire swirled and spat, billowing smoke that twisted into shapes of horrible looking beasts.

The raven choir continued. The creatures on the ground surrounded the woman and chanted her name. Louder and louder only two words could be heard, 'Queen Magh, Queen Magh'

9

Crossing the Bog

Licked and nudged by Greyfriars, Benjamin woke up slightly disturbed.

''lo, little guy,' mumbled Benjamin sleepily, stroking the soft fur of the little animal. He forced his eyelids open as he nuzzled into Greyfriars' neck. 'Don't reckon Gideon would let you come with us, do you?' Benjamin got up and changed quickly into the travelling boots, tunic, trousers and cloak that had been laid out for him. With a look around, he left his bedroom for the last time.

'How was your sleep?' Gideon asked when Benjamin entered the front room.

Benjamin scratched his head. 'Okay, I guess. I kept dreaming of a black raven and a big fire.'

Gideon's eyes flashed to Benjamin. 'Were those the only two things you saw in your dream?'

'Yeah,' Benjamin said timidly after looking at Gideon's expression.

Gideon's face softened, 'I'm sure it was just from our late night meeting.'

After breakfast and a quick pep talk from Gideon, they all went through the waterfall, emerging next to the river. The water thundered down around Benjamin as he passed through, but not so much as a drop fell on him. He even managed to walk on the slippery rocks without falling.

Once on the other side of the waterfall, Benjamin strained to see across the river through the haze.

'It's really foggy this morning,' he said. He silently hoped the fog would be enough to delay their start by a day or two.

'I'm afraid that your days of seeing the sun are over for the time being,' replied Gideon. 'The haze lingers as a reminder of Magh. It has not yet crossed over Water's Hyde and into the West of Meridia, but if you complete your journey, then Meridia will surely be lost.'

Benjamin looked across the river to where the thick cloud hung heavy like a lead blanket over the Bogwumps.

'It may be wise to keep close to the river,' Gideon said to Jeems as he helped Benjamin with his pack. Benjamin gasped slightly, his knees bending under the weight on his back.

'This will get lighter, right?' groaned Benjamin. Gideon came around to face Benjamin and put his staff into his hand.

'Be safe. The oracle of a child's return is well known.' Gideon touched the side of Benjamin's face. 'My dear boy, how very brave you are, to take all of this in and be so trusting in so little time. Good luck, and take care.'

Benjamin felt a lump well up in his throat as he tried to say goodbye. There was a part of him that felt lost because

Gideon wasn't coming. But why? He hadn't known Gideon that long, had he? There was something so strangely familiar about him, something that Benjamin had been trying to figure out since their first meeting.

With a final farewell to Jeems and Primrose, Gideon shimmered away, muttering about having to attend to something on the other side of Meridia. They trudged along the river bank in the misty morning air, talking and laughing until noon. After lunch they continued on until nightfall, and Benjamin helped Jeems set up camp for the night.

The next morning the fog chilled the air. The dampness made its way into Benjamin's bones and he shivered uncontrollably.

'Reckon we'll be leavin' the riverside terday an' crossin' over the fields ter the bog.' Jeems coughed and fanned thick smoke away from his face. The fires had been getting harder to light due to the dampness in the air. Lost behind black smoke, Benjamin coughed.

'I don't think it's going to start,' said Benjamin, his eyes watering from the smoke. 'Even Primrose is struggling to breathe fire.'

'Best just ter get movin' on, then. Here, catch,' said Jeems, throwing Benjamin an apple. Benjamin could hear the downhearted tone in Jeems' voice. It was hard be cheery in such dreary weather. The closer they got to the bog the greyer and damper the air became. The sun had been lost behind the thick low lying cloud that now surrounded them.

Jeems led the way as the three of them trudged on over the grass, the ground thicker and spongier with every step. 'S'not far now,' Jeems called back. 'Just the bog is just up ahead, so it is.'

Their boots made a squelching sound as they approached the edge of the water. Benjamin's eyes adjusted to the dimness, and he could see trees sticking out from the mud. When they finally reached the bog, Jeems stopped a few feet away from the shore.

'Wait 'ere,' he muttered and turned to his right, vanishing in the thick, low-lying cloud that covered the bog.

Benjamin went to the water's edge. The water was black, with no hope of seeing to the bottom. It was still and undisturbed - there was no movement at all.

A dragging sound made Benjamin turn around to where Jeems had disappeared earlier. Benjamin could barcly make out the shape of Jeems struggling with something long and heavy. As Jeems came closer, Benjamin saw him dragging a long boat with a point at either end, like a kayak but with a hollowed out middle.

'What's that?' asked Benjamin.

'It's me knu. Made it meself from one o' them trees.' Jeems pointed over to some tall trees off to the side of the bog's edge. The white bark that covered the trees was the same as the outside of the knu. Benjamin noticed that the shimmering whiteness of the bark gave them their only light. Jeems set the knu silently in the water. As they settled in, Benjamin spotted some water coming in. He panicked and put his staff in the water to bring them back to shore.

'Don' disturb the water. The knu will go by itself,' whispered Jeems hoarsely. 'And don't worry 'bout the water in the boat, it's only a few drops.'

The knu glided on its own silently through the bog. To the left a shot of steam hissed up from the water.

'Bog gas,' muttered Jeems. 'Better hope we don't get a shot of it o'er here. One shot will knock ya out cold, so it will. Puts ya inter an eternal nightmare.'

The knu continued through the bog. Benjamin thought he felt a slight bump, and looked down to make sure they weren't taking in any more water. As he did, a long, slimy finger came through a small crack in the side of the boat.

'What's that?' startled, Benjamin scrambled to the other end of the boat, causing it to rock wildly.

'Hey, hey stop that, ya'll tip us!' ordered Jeems. 'Whadda think yer doin'? There's nothin' there.'

'I saw something. It looked like a finger,' Benjamin gasped.

'Maybe ya was just imaginin' it, or thought ya saw summat ya didn't. It's dark in here an' all,' Jeems said reassuringly. 'Don't go pullin' a stunt like that again or we'll both end up in the water, and believe me, that water is not a place ya'd want ter end up in.'

Benjamin settled down once more. Before long, they came across blue frogs of various sizes sitting on mounds of weed and mud that were dotted across the water. The knu drifted by a rather large frog and Benjamin took a closer look.

'That's a tog, that is, an' there ain't nothin' grand about it. One bite an' yer a goner,' Jeems said matter of factly. In an instant the frog jumped off its mound into the water. Within seconds it climbed back up with a fish twice its own size in its mouth. It wasn't until then that Benjamin noticed the frog's razor sharp teeth and blue tongue. He leaned over the knu to watch the frog more closely when a slight ripple in the water caught his eye.

He strained his eyes and bowed his head closer to the water until he could see the outline of a very skinny woman's face. Her open eyes were round and wide and her hair was green and stringy, floating along the side of her head. She swam towards him quickly.

The next thing Benjamin heard was a loud shriek and a giant splash as he was grabbed around the neck by twelve long slimy fingers. He stared in to the face of the gaunt looking green woman who had just captured him. Her mouth was open and two long fangs covered in green swamp scum hung from a crowded mouthful of very sharp teeth. Benjamin's head snapped back as he was pulled out of the boat and down under the water.

Benjamin struggled wildly, which just made her tighten her grip and her talon-like nails pierced his shoulder. He felt woozy as she brought him down to a bed of weeds on the floor of the bog. Forcing his eyes open, Benjamin noticed that the water around him was not as black as the water above. He saw bones of fish and small children littered over the floor of her den. Benjamin continued to struggle, but he knew he needed to breathe soon. In desperation he groped around on the bog floor with his free hand until he found a large, sharp bone. With his last ounce of strength, he swung the bone at his captor, striking her arm. Black liquid oozed out of her and he heard a garbled shriek as she let go and swam away.

His head pounded as Benjamin fought his way back up to the surface. His shoulder burned with pain, causing his arm to feel heavy and useless. His heart felt like it was going to go through his chest. His head was getting heavy and his lungs felt as though they were going to explode. With one arm he swam up towards the knu floating above. The water felt thicker with every stroke. The last thing he saw was a hand coming down towards him before his eyes closed and his head flopped forward.

Benjamin fought to open his eyes. He could feel someone trying to shake him awake, could hear Jeems' voice off in the distance: 'Stay with me, don't go ter sleep.' He barely felt the bump as the knu docked and Jeems dragged his limp body on to the shore. In the distance, he could hear the hissing and spitting of the creature that had grabbed him.

Once again, Benjamin heard the faraway sound of Jeems'. 'He's hurt, Medrim. A greenling's gone an' nabbed him. Took him right outta the boat!'

Benjamin opened his eyes. His vision was blurred but he thought he saw two dark eyes surrounded by thick, long black hair. He heard a rattle in front of him and saw two balls like coconuts tied to a staff being shaken around him.

'Into the depths he falls,' said a gruff voice he didn't recognise.

As Benjamin gasped for breath, everything suddenly went black.

****

In the darkness that followed,   Benjamin saw himself as a baby on a boat, the sound of the water slapped against the sides. ... His eyes flinched against the bright sunlight. ... A man with a tatty old hat bent over him and smiled. ...

The man picked him up .... he said something that Benjamin couldn't understand....the floor of the boat was covered in freshly caught fish ....Benjamin crinkled his nose at the smell.

....instantly huge black clouds covered the sun and a cold, harsh wind came up.... the man's eyes filled with fear... rain like icy daggers began pelting down... the wind whistled 'give me the boy'... the man let out a loud 'no!'... the waves grew.... they turned into snakes heads and crashed over the boat.... Benjamin was swallowed by one of the snakes...he plunged into the water ...

Benjamin's eyes shot open. Drenched with sweat, he struggled to focus. He looked around and tried to figure out where he was. He was so disturbed by his dream, he had forgotten for a moment what had happened in the bog.

'Jeems? Primrose?' Benjamin tried to talk but only managed a whisper. His throat felt like sandpaper and he winced when he swallowed. He tried to sit up, but was knocked back down by the pain in his shoulder.

Rubbing his shoulder, he looked around curiously. He was lying on an overstuffed mattress made out of leaves. The rounded hut he was in was made out of sticks and stuck together with mud. There was a small bowl beside him containing yellow liquid.

Jeems, who was sleeping against one of the walls, woke up with a snort. 'Aye. Yer awake, so ya are. Knew ya'd pull through. I told ol' Medrim ya'd be awright.' Grinning, he went over and knelt beside Benjamin.

'I – I had a horrible dream. I was a baby...' Benjamin couldn't bear to go on. 'I'm so thirsty.'

'Course ya are. Here, drink this,' Jeems handed him a wooden cup. 'This'll see ya better in no time.'

Benjamin drank the yellow liquid. It felt cool and refreshing as it went down his throat.

'Essence of elicampe,' said Jeems directly. 'Best thing ter fight against a greenling wound. The elicampe grows wild in Nygirth Forest, but I wouldn't have known where ter look fer it 'round here. Good thing Medrim keeps his stocks up.'

'Medrim?' Benjamin asked as he swallowed the last of the yellow juice. 'Who's he?'

'The Bogwump who saved ya,' replied Jeems. 'Got ya ter him just in time, I did. I thought ya was a goner when that greenling pulled ya from the boat. I'm serprised ya came back up ter the surface, greenlings don't normally lose hold of summat once they get 'em.'

Benjamin told Jeems what had happened, how she had torn into his shoulder and what he had done to free himself. Jeems let out a low whistle.

'What? asked Benjamin.

'Well, like ya saw, that greenling's caught loads in the past. Every'un knows that a greenling wound makes ya go stiff. I've never heard of no'un bein' able ter get away from a greenling. Maybe it's inside ya, but summat kept ya from freezin' up an' turnin' green.' Jeems refilled Benjamin's cup and passed it to him.

'Thanks,' said Benjamin, taking another gulp. 'It happened so fast, I don't think there was time for me to go stiff.'

Jeems shook his head. 'I dunno, greenling's are as quick as lightnin'. An' there's a reason ya escaped. That's why Gideon called ya here, and if there's one thing I know it's that Gideon don't do nothin' fer no good reason.'

The two friends sat in silence. Benjamin clutched his rumbling stomach.

'Let's get outta here an' find ya summat ter eat,' said Jeems.

Benjamin let Jeems help him up and out of the stick hut. Once outside, Benjamin noticed that the bog was brighter than when he and Jeems had crossed it. Benjamin and Jeems weaved through a number of people who scuttled around with sticks, large leaves and other small tools. The shore of the bog was lined with huts exactly like the one he had just come out of. In front of each hut small fires glowed from round fire pits. Wooden bowls and plates lay strewn on the ground.

'Who are these, these ...' Benjamin found it hard to describe them.

'These are Bogwumps,' replied Jeems.

All around the shore of the bog Benjamin could see the Bogwumps busy at work. They were short and slender with muscular arms and legs. Some walked in and out of the bog with pails of water. Others had armfuls of black fish. Most of them went right underwater but their hair did not get wet no matter how long they waded in the murky bog. The water from the bog dried quickly from their reddish-brown skin.

Benjamin felt something poke his right leg. He looked down to see a Bogwump child staring up at him. The child held up a banana leaf with a mound of delicious looking fruits on it.

'Thank you, Moonbeam,' said Jeems and he took the leaf from the little girl who scuttled away, giggling. He gave some to Benjamin and then laid the leaf on a stone. Benjamin ate quickly and hungrily, not stopping to wipe drips away from his chin.

Benjamin was just about to take some more when Jeems nudged his arm and said, 'C'mon, I reckon Medrim and the Chief will want ter see ya.'

Benjamin and Jeems walked a short distance through the encampment until they came to a hut that was slightly bigger than the rest. The outside of the hut was decorated with leaves and what looked like nuts that had been strung together. Skulls of the scary frogs that Jeems called togs rested on top of bamboo rods and lined the walkway to the door.

Inside the hut were a number of adult Bogwumps, but two larger Bogwumps stood out above the rest. The muttering stopped as Benjamin entered, and all but the two larger Bogwumps cleared out of the hut. They looked much like the rest, although the one wore a hat shaped like the head of a bison. The other one had a headband of bones and leaves that came down around his ears and to a point in the middle of his forehead. Around his neck hung a string of tog skulls and teeth.

'Welcome,' said the Bogwump with the bison hat. 'I am Chief Thuglot. This is Medrim, our healer.' The one with the headband bowed his head slightly. 'Happy we are to see you. Food is what you need. The night eye has watched over us thrice since you fell into the dark sleep.'

Benjamin looked quizzically at Jeems, who leaned over to him and whispered, 'Ya've bin sleepin' fer three days.'

Benjamin sat on the floor next to a low table full of the same food he had seen the other Bogwumps get from the bog. Noticing the anxious look on Benjamin's face, Medrim said in a hoarse voice, 'The bog is our life source. Poison it is to others, yet food to us and those we welcome. Eat.'

Benjamin eyed a small fish that had been fried with its tail still on. His hunger had got the best of him, and with his eyes closed he bit into it, surprised at the taste. He gathered up the nerve to try more and more until he had eaten twice as much as he thought possible.

After they finished eating, Thuglot shifted on his cushion and prepared to speak.

'Medrim says you are healed.' Thuglot's voice was low and quiet. 'This is good.'

'I thought I was a goner,' replied Benjamin. 'It wasn't until I –'

Benjamin stopped suddenly and looked at Thuglot. He wasn't sure how Thuglot would react if he knew that Benjamin had to hurt the greenling to free himself. Gideon had told him that the Bogwumps didn't like to see any creature come to harm.

'Others before you have fallen to the greenling. You survived when no other has. I sense in you a strength not often seen.'

'I've heard,' Benjamin said nervously and rubbed his shoulder.

Thuglot continued as if he hadn't heard him, 'It is our wisdom you seek. Wisdom given to us as a gift since we first walked on Meridia. Gifts that are protected by the bog.' Thuglot motioned outside the hut, stopped talking and rested his hands on his crossed knees.

After a few moments, Benjamin spoke up. 'I'm supposed to see if I can read the oracle and then, well - I don't know what will happen after that.'

Thuglot was silent for a moment before addressing Benjamin once more. 'It is for the bog to decide if you are the one intended. The oracle was sent to us long before the North darkness lingered. You must raise the oracle to begin your journey. If you raise it, this will tell Meridia you have come.'

Benjamin crinkled his eyebrows and frowned. 'I'm not sure I want anyone else to know I'm here,' Benjamin said as he thought back to the furls and the greenling.

Thuglot raised his hands in protest. 'To hide is the way of the weak. Easier, yes, but not the intended way. Boldness and inner strength will assist you in the storms you must weather to complete your journey. To depart from the way intended will bring strife.'

'But then Magh will know I'm here,' reasoned Benjamin.

Thuglot nodded slowly. 'It is for you to decide,' he answered and bowed his head.

Before Benjamin could continue the door swung open and he turned to see Gideon crouching down to get through the doorway.

'Gideon – you're here!' Benjamin said loudly as he stood up to greet him.

Gideon studied Benjamin's face closely before he said affectionately, 'You didn't think I would miss your raising ceremony, did you?'

10

The Raising Ceremony

Gideon sat down on the other side of Thuglot and waited for Benjamin to settle before he asked, 'What have I missed?'

'Thuglot was just talkin' ter Benjermin 'bout the oracle, is all,' said Jeems in a hoarse voice. He hadn't slept well since Benjamin had been hurt and it was starting to show.

'Ah, yes, the oracle.' Gideon turned to Benjamin. 'I trust, then, that Thuglot has told you that raising the oracle will alert Magh of your presence in Meridia?'

Benjamin nodded.

Gideon fixed his gaze downwards. 'Knowing that, are you still prepared to go ahead with raising it?'

Benjamin thought for a moment. The only alternative was to go back to Hadley Priest and for some reason he felt strangely at home in Meridia. 'Yeah,' he said, picking at the blades of grass that were poking up through the hut floor. 'I'll do it.' Benjamin turned his head and looked between Gideon and Thuglot. 'But after that, then what?'

'Do you remember the scales I showed you at Water's Hyde?' Gideon asked.

Benjamin nodded.

'As you saw, the scales are weighing evenly against each other. The only way to shift the scales towards good is to get the four leagues that were hidden years ago. Once they are back in the Arcrux and placed in the scale, evil in Meridia will be conquered once again.'

'Uh – leagues?' Benjamin said, puzzled.

'There are four leagues in all – each one representing the elements which make up Meridia. The first league is the seeds from the Vie tree. You will need to find the leagues, in turn, and return them to them to the Arcrux.'

Benjamin sat in silence, not sure what to say. It was very difficult when you didn't really know what you were getting into, Benjamin thought. However, he managed to utter a very faint, 'Okay.'

Thuglot, who hadn't said anything since Gideon had arrived, spoke up. 'The first of four, the Earth League. It is buried in the base of the Great Tree, guarded by the creatures of Wyldewych. It is to the giant, Er, you must go.'

Benjamin felt slightly nervous at the mention of giants and looked at Jeems. Jeems sat casually and didn't look at all bothered. Benjamin took a deep breath and tried to relax.

Gideon continued, 'There is a giant that helps to guard the league named Er. The league, as Thuglot said, is at the very roots of the Vie tree. There is one hole in the tree where you can enter it to get to its roots. There is only one hole that goes through the centre of its trunk. It was left after the tree gave me its branch to make your staff.' Gideon motioned to Benjamin's staff that was lying on the ground next to him. 'It is unlike any other knot or hole in the tree and the way down is streaked with gold.'

Benjamin looked at his staff. There was a gold shimmer to the wood and for the first time he saw the outlines of faces that were carved in it. Knowing that everyone was looking at him, Benjamin kept his eyes fixed on the staff.

'Benjamin,' Gideon spoke very gently. 'I am in no doubt there will be obstacles in your path. Aside from Er, Wyldewych is another example of what Magh has done to try and stop you getting to the leagues. The Vie tree, once alive and flourishing, now stands wilted. Behind Wyldewych it towers, naked and dry, stripped of its life. Wyldewych was placed before it to stop people getting to the tree. It is a mass of thorned bushes and vines with creatures that were created for destruction. The evils that lie in it are there not only to stop you from getting to the league – but to stop you once and for all.'

Benjamin shifted uncomfortably and held his staff in his hands. He had come too far to turn back now. And besides, he thought, there was still the oracle – maybe Gideon made a mistake and Benjamin would be on his way back to Hester and the others. But something told him that Gideon knew exactly what he was doing.

Thuglot lifted his head and spoke once again. 'Let us not dwell on what is yet to come. A ceremony there is to prepare.'

Benjamin followed Jeems out and they went towards Primrose who was sharpening her claws on some rocks. Jeems sat on the rock next to Primrose and said casually, 'Don' ya worry 'bout ol' Er. Between the three 'o us we'll git ya past him, Wyldewych an' all.' His reassuring voice made Benjamin smile.

'Thanks,' he said dryly. 'So what is a raising ceremony?'

'Oh yeah. Well, it's a big thing, feast an' all. Like Thuglot said, yer supposed ter read the oracle fer yerself. So ya have ter go through the bog and the like.' Jeems cleared his throat. 'Uh – Gideon can tell ya more.' Quick to change the subject, Jeems looked around and said, 'Let's go see if these folk need any help.'

The rest of the day was spent preparing for the ceremony. Benjamin had become a local hero, and all the Bogwumps wanted to meet him. He was ferried from one hut to another, shaking hands and eating strange-looking food.

'They say you escaped the greenling,' gushed a young Bogwump with black hair and a dimple on his right cheek.

'Never has she missed,' said the women to each other as they stirred large pots of food over open fires.

The whole thing struck Benjamin as odd, because nobody had ever talked about him like this before. Normally when people talked about him it was about things he couldn't do – but this was totally different. By the end of the day he was so happy to be popular he had almost forgotten about the raising ceremony.

He went into Thuglot's hut with a huge grin on his face. Gideon was dressed in shiny bronze robes, and smiled at Benjamin as he came in.

'It is time,' said Thuglot. He scuttled past Benjamin, patting his shoulder as he left.. The top of his hat barely made it through.

'Here is a sign of friendship to the Bogwumps.' Medrim said and gently placed a necklace of tog skulls and teeth around Benjamin's neck. 'All who raise an oracle have eternal service from us.'

'Thanks,' muttered Benjamin. He looked down at the bones and teeth around his neck and tried not to shudder.

Outside, Benjamin could hear the scuffle of feet as one by one all the Bogwumps came out of their huts for the ceremony. Their excited murmuring filled the air.

'Benjamin,' Gideon began. He held a small, flat stone in his hand. 'The oracle will only show itself to the one who is meant to hear it. If you have doubt or show weakness, the oracle will not rise. And that, Benjamin, would put the future of Meridia in peril.'

'What if I'm not the one?' Benjamin asked nervously. 'What if I try but I'm not the one?'

'There was one who did try to raise an oracle that they were not intended to see.' Gideon spoke in a soft tone. 'They were consumed by the bog, never to be seen again. But alas, that was during a darker time than we are in even now, and evil was everywhere.'

Benjamin was sure he could see a tear in Gideon's eye and looked away. Gideon pushed the stone into Benjamin's hand and wrapped his fingers around it.

'You must say the verse on this stone to raise the oracle. Do not say it before it is time, and you must say it firmly. Remember, Benjamin, this oracle is about you – you are meant to know it.'

Gideon left Benjamin alone in the hut. What was he supposed to do now? Was it time to say the verse? Benjamin looked down at the stone – there was nothing on it.

'Oh no,' he groaned. 'He gave me the wrong one.' Benjamin paced the length of the hut. Maybe he should have followed Gideon out. Were they waiting for him? Or worse, had they left without him?

Benjamin made his way to the door. It swung open by itself when he approached it. He heard drums outside and the low murmur of voices. Straightening up, Benjamin took a deep breath and stepped outside.

It was as if he had walked into a totally different world. The Bogwump encampment had been transformed right under Benjamin's nose. The bamboo poles that lined the path to Thuglot's hut were ablaze with fire. Bamboo poles just like them traced the entire bog, flickering through the trees in the distance. All of the little campfires were much higher and hotter than earlier that day. To the right Benjamin saw a huge bonfire. All the Bogwumps, including Jeems and Gideon, were gathered in a circle around it. Primrose had been used as the firestarter and was lying to the side with smoke coming out of her nostrils, her tongue hanging out. Amongst the crowd was a space left open large enough for one person.

Benjamin walked down the path towards the bonfire. The drummers, nestled out of sight around the bog, hummed and beat their drums in time to his steps. The Bogwump children, playful and full of life earlier, looked serious and earnest as they cuddled into their mothers. The group parted to let Benjamin through as he approached and took his place between Gideon and Jeems. He saw Thuglot across the blaze of the fire in front of him.

'Gideon,' Benjamin whispered, 'Gideon, you gave me the wrong stone. There's nothing on this one.'

Gideon stared into the fire.

'Gideon,' he hissed a bit louder. 'The stone you gave me is blank. You gave me the –'

All of a sudden the drums stopped and Thuglot stood up and raised his hands. He walked around to where Benjamin stood and placed another necklace of tog teeth and dried fruit around his neck.

'Many years have we lived in our cloud, watching the good lands be taken by the darkness, but no more.'

A small stringed instrument began to play. Thuglot motioned for everybody to sit down. 'A great story there is to be told of how we have been taken into shadow.' Thuglot threw a small pinch of powder in the fire, which caused it to leap and dance. Thuglot spoke with the flames flickering in time.

'Years ago, in the days of my ancestors, the shadow was cast away. But many were lost, and destruction lingered. Over time, the battle was forgotten, and Meridia did not pay attention to the growing gloom in the North. The will of men grew weak as sinister creatures began to move through the land once again.'

Benjamin scanned the group as Thuglot spoke. All eyes were on the Bogwump chief. Even Primrose was listening intently.

Thuglot continued. 'Men were blinded by a desire for power, and let themselves be deceived. All seemed lost, and the Bogwumps lay forgotten, covered in the mist surrounding the bog. The promise once spoken was cast aside, and despair turned into fear. Many fell to the dark shadows.'

Thuglot's eyes rested on Benjamin. 'But the oracles that we speak are true. One speaks of a child to come as beacon, but he must prove that his heart is just to release all people from the grip of evil.'

Benjamin looked away from Thuglot and watched the flames. Quite high and active when Thuglot was speaking, they had plunged back into the fire when he stopped.

'But now a new season is upon us,' Thuglot turned to Benjamin. 'It is time to raise the oracle. The way is found in the fire.' Thuglot's voice rose over the crowd.

Thuglot motioned Benjamin towards the raging fire. Benjamin inched towards it, unsure of what he was supposed to do. He looked around … should he tell them there was nothing on the stone? He caught Jeems' eye. Jeems picked up a stone and motioned for Benjamin to put his hand in the fire.

'What?' Benjamin mouthed silently. 'Are you mad?'

He looked at Gideon, who stared at him intently. Benjamin swallowed hard. Nobody had told him that he was meant to get his hand burned off. The heat of the fire was intense. Benjamin felt sweat slide down his back and the side of his face.

You must do this with authority… it is yours to hear…' Benjamin heard Gideon's words playing over and over again in his mind. He wrapped his fingers around the stone Gideon had given him and thrust it into the fire. He closed his eyes and clenched his teeth. He could feel it – it was horrible, it was terrible, it was … it was… painless.

His mouth wide open, Benjamin watched the flames lick his tightly clenched hand. After a few moments he pulled it out and looked at the stone. Writing, in small green lettering, had formed on the flat stone. He turned it over and then back again, surprised at how cool it was. Reading the verse, he found his voice. 'The pro –' Thuglot silenced him.

'The oracle is in the bog. Go to its shores.'

With a wave of Thuglot's hand the crowd parted, giving Benjamin a clear path to the bog. With great trepidation, Benjamin advanced towards the shore. He stood with his back to the crowd, which had now closed in around him.

'It is time,' said Thuglot softly.

Benjamin looked down at the stone. The words shone bright green in the firelight. He read them over a few times to himself, cleared his throat and began to call the oracle:

The promise once made is now to be; the truth is told. I set you free.

The words came out loud and clear. Slightly shocked, Benjamin looked around to see if anyone else had noticed how loudly he said it. Then he heard a low rumble coming from the bog.

He turned to the bog and saw the water bubble up slowly in the very centre. Above the bog, the thick cloud parted and the moonlight burned through, shining directly into the centre of the bog. At Benjamin's feet the water rushed towards the centre of the bog, creating a path to the bubbling water. It parted the bog and made walls of water on either side that towered over Benjamin.

The rushing water reached the centre and collided with the bubbles to create a whirlpool. From the mouth of the whirlpool a huge stone gradually rose on a pillar of water. It revolved around slowly, rising until it stopped about three feet in the air, the pillar of water underneath it held it in place.

Benjamin began to walk through the bog towards the stone. Not even his fear of another greenling could stop him. The spray from the walls of water was intense and he had trouble seeing. The mud on the bog floor was thick and a few times he struggled to free his feet. Even if I do read this oracle I might get stuck in the mud and drown, he kept thinking. This and a million other things raced through his head as he reached the pillar of water and looked at the huge stone's blank face.

'Now what?' he muttered as he searched the stone for a clue as to what to do next.

Just as Benjamin was beginning to believe that he had messed up somewhere along the way, letters started to appear on the stone as they had done with the little rock that was still in his hand. He watched as the letters formed themselves into words - words that had been submerged for many, many years.

In presentation unremarkable he comes. He will cast away the one who destroys. He will be known by his just heart that cannot be turned. People will have a new hope.

Benjamin had just enough time to read it through twice before the words vanished back into the stone. As quickly as Benjamin could blink, the stone started to lower itself into the bog. Taking the cue, Benjamin turned and headed towards the shore, the water falling back into the bog just as he reached the shore. The bog once again stood silent and still, the moon swallowed by the cloud. He stood on the shore, panting and dripping wet, his hand wrapped tightly around the small stone Gideon had given him. He turned to look at the group behind him who started to cheer.

An enormous feast and celebration followed Benjamin's raising ceremony. Music played, people danced and food was everywhere as the entire encampment came alive. Still stunned by what he had just done, Benjamin sat a few feet away from the group watching Gideon as he tried to play a strange-looking brass instrument called a chubaa. Drying himself by a small fire, Benjamin was soon joined by Gideon who had passed the chubaa on to Jeems and was in especially good spirits.

'Gideon,' Benjamin began, 'how come no one's asked me what the oracle said?'

'That is because it's not for them to know.' Gideon shifted to have a better view of the band. 'You may remember, Benjamin that earlier this evening I told you that this oracle was meant for you.'

Benjamin nodded.

'And yours it is.'

Benjamin wrinkled his nose in confusion. 'So I have to keep it to myself?'

'It would be wise for you not to share it with many people, but it is yours to share. It has been widely known for many years that an oracle existed about a child. There is also some who thought that the same oracle also spoke of the child saving Meridia from the hands of evil. Few, however, knows what it actually says. The most important thing to remember is that those words hold a great deal of foresight. You will need to be careful about whom you choose to share it with. Having said that, I am in no doubt that you are struggling to make sense of it. I will impress upon you now that it will be clearer in time.'

'To be honest, I can hardly remember what it said. I only had time to read it through twice and there were some words I'd never seen before.'

Gideon cracked a nut with his teeth. 'Mm, I think you will find that the small stone I gave you may be of some use to you once again.' Gideon smacked his lips. 'I do like these flognuts.'

Benjamin looked at the small stone he still had in his hand. In place of the writing he spoke to call the oracle out of the water, was the oracle itself in the same green writing.

'It will only glow when warmed by the heat of your hand,' he heard Gideon say softly in his ear. 'But guard it well all the same. Magh's influence increases daily and she would do anything to read what is written on that stone.'

Just as Benjamin decided to tell Gideon about his latest dream, loud shouts came from behind the huts. Three Bogwump guards rushed past Benjamin and Gideon, hauling what looked like a big black animal over their shoulders.

The guards approached Thuglot, who reacted with surprise and anger at the dead creature. Gideon left Benjamin's side instantly and reappeared next to Thuglot on the other side of the encampment. Jeems met Benjamin on his way towards the growing crowd, and by the time they got close the creature was slumped on the ground.

It was the biggest, blackest raven Benjamin had ever seen before in his life. It was at least the size of a small Bogwump and very deep black. Just looking at it gave Benjamin an eerie feeling and he had to look away.

'The beast was flying overhead, trying to catch the rays of the moon. Searching, it was. Searching for a way through the cloud.' The guard panted hard as he spoke.

The murmurs in the crowd and the wide-eyed response of both Thuglot and Gideon told Benjamin that this was not a good sign.

'What happened to it?' Benjamin asked Jeems, looking away in disgust.

'Reckon them guards got it with one o' their tog's teeth darts.' Jeems bent down to get a closer look. 'Look 'ere, ya can see the blue dart in the belly.' He pointed to a small dart in its huge underside.

'He looks just like the one I dreamt about,' Benjamin said to himself.

'Did ya say summat?' Jeems asked.

'Er – no. Just that it's really big.' Benjamin responded.

Gideon and Thuglot spoke quickly and quietly with one another. Thuglot nodded his head and then said to his guards, 'You have protected your people well. The greenling that was robbed of her catch before has been on a rock on the far side of the bog. Give her this offering with our thanks.'

With a nod of their heads, two guards waded out into the bog with the large bird strung across their shoulders. The hissing and gurgles that came from the mist moments later was a clear signal to the Bogwump chief that the greenling was happy. With the party mood broken, everyone started to return to their huts.

Inside his hut, Benjamin turned restlessly in his bed of straw and leaves. Jeems was already snoring, but Benjamin could not sleep.

'Jeems, Jeems, are you awake?'

'Humph,' snorted Jeems. 'Not really. Wot d'yer need?'

'What was the big deal with that raven? Why was everyone so upset about it?'

Jeems propped himself up on his elbow. 'That raven was a spy from Magh, more likely than not.'

'Magh?' Benjamin's eyes widened. Does she already know I'm here?'

'Maybe she does, maybe it was just flyin' by an' saw the moon burn through the cloud.' Jeems shifted uncomfortably in his bed. 'Every'un 'round here knows that this 'ere cloud only breaks fer a raisin' ceremony.' He shrugged and shook his head once. 'Hard ter say.'

'It was huge,' Benjamin said. He really liked Jeems, but he wasn't a big talker, and Benjamin got the feeling that he knew much more than what he was letting on.

'They all are. I've seen bigger. Their leader is – well.' Jeems sized up Benjamin with his eyes. 'I reckon their leader is as big as ya.' And with that Jeems let out a huge yawn and nestled back down under his covers. 'Don' matter none now anyways. It's dead. G'night.'

'Good night,' said Benjamin reluctantly.

Benjamin lay awake, tossing and turning. The encampment was silent, the only noise being the odd crackling of the dying fires that dotted the shores. Benjamin focused on the silence, his mind once again racing with questions. If Magh had sent the raven, she would be expecting it back, wouldn't she? How did she know to send it here? The questions were never-ending.

The sounds of scuffling feet outside his hut made Benjamin sit up. He rose slowly and crept to the door to see who was outside. Peeking through the door, Benjamin saw Gideon in the dim firelight. He was bent down, gathering up a small pile of sand and dirt from the ground that he scooped into his cupped hands. He then turned his back to Benjamin, blocking his view. Benjamin strained his neck to see what Gideon was doing. Suddenly and as if by magic, wings sprang out from Gideon's waist, making Benjamin stumble back in surprise. Gideon turned around again to face Benjamin who ducked behind the door. He peered out and saw Gideon holding a large raven in his hands. It looked exactly like the one the Bogwumps had caught earlier that night. Gideon whispered something to it and then let it go. The raven hung suspended over its creator for a moment before flying up and out of the cloud.

Benjamin lay back down, more awake and full of questions than before. What had Gideon done? Why would he create another spy for Magh? Crazy thoughts and mad ideas swam around Benjamin's head until he drifted off to sleep.

11

Knocking Rocks

The next morning, it wasn't long after he woke up that Benjamin realised Gideon had already left the Bogwump camp. He tried to ignore the sinking feeling in the pit of his stomach when he thought of Gideon making that raven. He turned his attention to the journey that lay ahead and sat down at the low table to a helping of dried fruits and flognuts. A few minutes later Jeems came walking around the corner of the hut towards the table. He sat down hard next to Benjamin, his right hand wrapped in strips of cloth.

'What happened?' Benjamin asked between mouthfuls of flognuts and flingleberries.

'Stupid dragon,' grumbled Jeems, tenderly cradling his bandaged hand and holding it close to his chest. 'I went ter check on her, ya know, make sure she was awright after last night. Well, I goes ter her an' she was still sleepin' so I gives her a pat on the back ter wake her up. She must've bin dreamin' or summat because she woke up with a fright an' before I knew it flames were shootin' out of her mouth, over me hand an' all.'

'That's gotta hurt,' Benjamin said, sucking in breath and shaking his head. 'Are we still going to be leaving then?' He braced himself in hopes that Jeems would say no.

'What's that? Oh, yeah, I'll get ol' Medrim ter sort me out in a bit.' Jeems piled fruit and nuts on to his plate with his good hand.

'Did you know that Gideon left?' Benjamin said through mouthfuls of bogwash cordial.

Jeems shook his head slightly. 'Na, but I can't say I'm serprised. He don't stick around anywheres too long, that Gideon. Busy I suppose. That, or he just gets plain restless.'

Benjamin watched Jeems for a while. Over the past few weeks, Benjamin realised just how loyal Jeems was to Gideon, so thought against telling him what he had seen last night. And even though Benjamin thought it was rude of Gideon to leave without saying goodbye, Jeems didn't seem too concerned about it. He decided not to let it bother him too much and packed up the bags while Jeems went to see Medrim. The packs were once again full of food and other stuff that the Bogwumps felt Benjamin and Jeems would need, including loads of bogwash cordial and a leather skinned pouch of essence of Elicampe.

All the Bogwumps gathered round to see Benjamin, Jeems and Primrose off. Jeems, now totally healed by some salve that Medrim had concocted, single-handedly swung his pack on to his back. Rather than cross the bog again, Jeems had planned to head behind the encampment and out towards the other side of Meridia. This was to Benjamin's relief.

Between the greenlings and the raising ceremony, he was happy to be seeing the last of the bog.

'To the giant you must go,' Thuglot said. 'Remember you must the words of Gideon – keep the oracle safe.'

Thuglot gave Benjamin a low bow, to which Benjamin responded with a not-so-low bow because he was afraid of falling over with his heavy pack. With a final wave, the three turned their back on the bog and left the safety of the cloud.

The only one who could see clearly through the dense fog was Primrose, so she led the way. Before long the air became warmer and drier, until at last they stepped out of the cloud and into the sunshine.

Standing tall and majestic before them was a group of mountains. Their snow-covered peaks pierced the clear blue sky with their jumbled array of jagged edges. Benjamin looked upon them and shivered with the thought of crossing their glacial peaks.

'Wow!' said Benjamin.

'Ya won't be sayin' that when we start ter climb them,' snorted Jeems.

'We're going up there?'

'Well, that's where ol' Er lives.' Jeems walked past Benjamin. 'Chin up. There's a small path, and we won't be goin' up as high as them peaks. It won't take long.'

Benjamin was glad to hear the last part. His stomach was telling him it was well past lunch, and the thought of a long journey made his knees feel weak.

Jeems remained thoughtful, staring at the mountains. 'I reckon it won't take us longer than two days.'

'Two days!' Benjamin dropped his rucksack and groaned deeply. 'Well, can we have some lunch first?'

'Too right,' agreed Jeems with a nod.

Sitting down to lunch on the finest food the Bogwumps had to offer, Benjamin remembered his first meal in Meridia – breakfast at Water's Hyde. That memory seemed so distant now.

'So, how long is this going to take, anyway?' asked Benjamin. 'I've already been gone for ages. Long enough for even Hester to notice.'

'Oh, don't ya worry 'bout that, mate. I'm sure Gideon will have that all under control. As fer the first question, well, I guess it'll take as long as it takes.' Jeems looked at Benjamin and grinned. 'Missin' home, are ya?'

Benjamin had not really given home a lot of thought. Although he had dreamed of Riley and Marcus, he couldn't say he missed being at Hadley Priest, or school for that matter. In fact, being in Meridia felt more like home than anywhere. For the first time he really felt as if he belonged somewhere.

Benjamin shrugged his shoulders. 'No, well, not really. I was just thinking that I'd already been away for a while, and they'd be noticing.'

'Suppose ya could talk to Gideon 'bout it, along with the dreams ya've had, the next time ya see him,' said Jeems, pulling a long strand of dried bog grass out of his teeth.

'Yeah, I'll do that,' then continued in a low voice, 'when we see him again. Whenever that is.'

They spent that first night at the base of the mountains. Jeems didn't think it was a good idea to start walking up the mountain pass so late in the afternoon. Instead he sent Primrose up to find a place to spend the next night.

'I don't like her flyin' far off during the day. She's a rare breed an' I wouldn't want her ter get hurt.'

The next day the three travellers set up the mountain at sunrise and it was soon very hard work for Benjamin. Sometimes the path was so narrow the slightest sideways movement caused rocks to come away and fall to the ground which, by the afternoon, Benjamin could hardly see. At one point it got so narrow that Benjamin and Jeems could do no more than put one foot in front of the other. Just when Benjamin thought he was going to fall off the side it widened and carried on for miles, allowing Benjamin and Jeems to walk side by side, laughing and chatting along the way. Primrose flew low and close to them, and Benjamin had almost forgotten where he was or what he was doing. That's when he heard a knocking sound come from the mountain.

'Did you hear that?' Benjamin asked Jeems.

'Hear what?' Jeems asked after taking a gulp of bogwash.

'That knocking sound,' said Benjamin. They stopped and Jeems had a look of concentration on his face as he strained his ears.

Everything was silent, save for the flapping of Primroses's wings. Jeems shook his head and shrugged. 'Can't say as I can. Maybe it's just some loose stones fallin' off the cliff.'

'It was like someone was knocking from inside the mountain,' Benjamin said, confused.

Jeems studied him with a concerned look. 'Ya heard knockin', ya say?'

Benjamin took a step back and pointed to where he thought he heard the noise. Jeems touched the side of the mountain. He put his ear to the stone and listened carefully. Benjamin opened his mouth to speak but Jeems put his hand up to stop him.

'There it is again!' Benjamin said, quite loudly this time. Jeems turned around and followed the sound a few feet. A faint knocking could be heard coming from inside the mountain. 'See, I told you,' Benjamin said proudly. 'I'm not hearing things –'

'We gotta get outta here,' Jeems said urgently. He grabbed Benjamin's arm and began to run along the mountainside.

Benjamin stumbled along. 'Wait. What was that knocking? Are we in trouble? Owwah!'

Something hard struck the back of Benjamin's head.

'Ow!' he screamed as something else hit him. He rubbed his head gingerly and looked up.

A stone the size of a man's fist hit the ground and rolled away over the cliff.

'Incoming!' Jeems yelled, diving on Benjamin to get him out of the way of a much larger boulder that came crashing down next to them.

Benjamin swallowed hard. 'Thanks.'

No sooner had they got up than the ground they were standing on started shaking. The shaking was followed by a rumbling and cracking noise. The knocking sound Benjamin had heard earlier was getting louder.

'Primrose, stay close!' ordered Jeems. Primrose had just landed safely when the rock face in front of them started to peel itself off the side of the mountain in one seamless motion.

Benjamin looked up to see a huge rock coming out of the cliff face with two arms, a body, two legs and feet. A thunderous roar filled the air and echoed through the mountains as fists made of rock came crashing down towards them.

'Khor,' gasped Jeems. He gaped at the moving mass of rock and tried to speak. It took him a moment to finally manage one work. 'Run!'

Benjamin, Jeems and Primrose scattered, dodging rocks twice their size as Khor's fists came crashing down. Terrified, Benjamin tried desperately to stay on his feet despite the mountain shaking enough to throw him off balance.

'Benjermin, over here!'

Benjamin turned to see Jeems through the dust that Khor had kicked up. He was waving him over to a crack in the mountain that he had found. Benjamin started going towards Jeems when one of Khor's fists came hurtling down within inches of him. The force of it sent him flying up onto a small, narrow ledge. As he landed, Benjamin hit his head hard against the mountain wall. He heard a crunching sound, followed by pain on his right side. He lay there, motionless for a moment, wondering if this was really happening.

Khor lumbered towards Benjamin, his heavy feet like thunder with every step he took. Staggering to get up, Benjamin steadied himself on the ledge and used his staff to support him. His eyes were open but everything was blurry. He closed them and shook his throbbing head, but it was no better. He could see the blurry shape of Khor coming closer as Benjamin tried to keep from passing out.

Khor let out another roar and looked down to where Jeems and Primrose were. Benjamin's watery eyes could just

111

make out the shapes of his friends, trying to draw Khor away from him. Primrose flew up around Khor's head, dropping small rocks and Jeems was at his feet, running around hollering. It bought Benjamin enough time to sit down on the ledge and think of what to do. What was he going to do? How were they going to get out of this? His body shook with every step Khor took and the entire mountain trembled.

His head swimming, Benjamin closed his eyes. Like a little voice in his head, the essence of elicampe came to mind. Of course, the healing power of the elicampe plant. He groped around in his pack for the skin of healing water that Medrim had given him, and breathed a sigh of relief when his hand found the soft skin pouch. Taking a big gulp, he rested his head against the cliff and closed his eyes.

Almost immediately, Benjamin felt his entire body getting warm. He opened his eyes clearly saw Khor simultaneously trying to stomp on Jeems and swat Primrose with his hand. Khor was using so much force to smash his hands and feet that his head began to wobble. Benjamin watched as Jeems ran in and around Khor's legs, dodging the deadly fists. He knew he should have been paralysed by fear, but he wasn't and instinctively let out a loud whooping sound to get Khor's attention.

A roar echoed through the mountains as Khor turned and advanced towards Benjamin. He came bounding over, his head, with two gaping holes for eyes, bouncing from side to side off his shoulders.

'Benjermin, wot'yer doin'?' Jeems yelled from below. 'He'll smash ya ter bits, he will!'

'I think - ' Benjamin gulped. 'I've got an idea!'

Benjamin looked at the staff in his hand and fixed his eyes on Khor. As the monster's hand came down towards him, Benjamin jumped on top of it and started to climb up Khor's arm to his shoulder. Confused, Khor swung his arm from side to side, trying to get Benjamin off him. Benjamin slid to and fro, his hands and arms aching with the strain of hanging on. Slowly he crept up to the base of Khor's neck and rose to his knees. He jammed his staff in between the rock's mighty neck and head, leaning on his staff with all his weight to pry Khor's head off of his shoulders.

Khor's head teetered, but not before he managed to knock Benjamin away from his staff. Falling knees first on Khor's shoulders, Benjamin managed to get up and was met by another blow from Khor's fist. The force knocked him towards his staff that was jammed between the rock monster's head and neck. As Benjamin was thrown against it, he grabbed hold of it and, with the help of the staff's strength prised Khor's head off his shoulders. Grunting and sweating, Benjamin gave one final yell as the huge head came crashing down.

Khor's headless body crashed and thrashed about. Benjamin hung on to Khor's neck as tightly as he could, knowing that if he were to let go it would probably mean his own death. Khor's body stumbled about while his head was still roaring a few feet away.

'Benjermin, get off, he's gonna go over the edge!' Jeems screamed from below as Khor stumbled dangerously close to the edge.

'Benjermin, jump!'

Benjamin looked down. He was about thirty storeys up from where Jeems was. He just caught a glimpse of Primrose flying up towards him when he fell over the edge with Khor.

Wind blew through his hair as Benjamin tried to climb up the huge falling rock. Freefalling, Khor's body twisted until Benjamin found himself between the rock and the mountain. The pack on his back bumped along the mountain face until it snagged on a rock that was jutting out. He let go of Khor and hung by the straps of his pack where they had caught on the mountain face. Khor met the ground below with a crash, disintegrating into a pile of rock dust. Up above, Benjamin swayed silently and gently in the breeze.

Jeems' voice rang out from the mountain ledge above. 'Benjermin! Benjermin! No! No! Primrose, go down there an' see if he's –' Jeems broke off and knelt down over the ledge. 'Oi. Benjermin.'

Benjamin looked up and saw Jeems' head poke out over the ledge. Within seconds, Primrose had flown down and was nuzzled into Benjamin, causing him to sway.

'Benjermin, well done, mate. Hang on an' we'll get ya back up.' Jeems threw down his pack and began rummaging through it. 'We'll get ya back up in no time.'

With the help of Primrose and Benjamin's rope, Benjamin was soon back up and on the path, close to the place Primrose had picked out for them to camp out when she went scouting the night before. By nightfall all three were lying by a brightly lit fire tending to their cuts and bruises.

'Pass me some o' that essence of elicampe, would ya,' Jeems moaned to Benjamin. His trouser leg was torn with a deep, long gash behind it.

Benjamin rooted around in his pack for what was left of the healing liquid. Shaking the pouch, he made a face as he passed it over.

'Sorry, there's not much left. I used some before when I was up on the ledge,' Benjamin said remorsefully.

Jeems opened the pouch and peered inside. 'Don't matter, ya don't need much,' he said, dripping a few drops over his leg.

Benjamin watched Jeems see to both himself and Primrose. Even though her scales were tough, she had managed to get quite a few cuts on the bottom of her feet.

'What was that thing? That *Khor*?' asked Benjamin.

115

'That was a rock monster,' replied Jeems, passing some food to Benjamin. 'Khor is – or - *was* the only rock monster in Meridia. Most of us, meself included, thought he was legend. I sure have been proved wrong.'

'How did he get here?' Benjamin asked.

'Well, they say he was created by some evil doer before Magh, after the leagues were hidden. Legend goes that Khor was created ter keep good folk from gettin' the Earth league. But some'un had ter call him out.' Jeems looked thoughtful and a little concerned.

The familiar feeling of being scared was back, and Benjamin's stomach tightened. 'Magh?' he asked.

Jeems shook his head. 'I dunno fer sure but I wouldn't be serprised.'

'Gideon said there was somebody else, like Magh's boss,' Benjamin pressed.

'That was long, long ago, before I was even born,' replied Jeems. 'Ya see, these leagues have bin gone fer, oh - ages. From what I know, things were goin' good in Meridia and then summat bad happened.'

'What?'

'Well, I don't know fer sure, but whatever it was shook Meridia up, so it did. Bad things were happenin' and it didn't seem like there was anythin' anybody could do about it. And then Magh showed up, sayin' things like *'the one who sent me'* and all that rubbish. She was bad ter the core, she was, and Meridia was in a bad way.'

'So what happened?' Benjamin was captivated.

'Well, then the Bogwump was sent the oracle, and - ' Jeems trailed off. He looked up in to the sky, like he in some kind of trance.

'What about the oracle?' Benjamin risked another question.

After a minute Jeems shook his head. 'Nah, I shouldn't be the one tellin' ya this. Isn't fer me ter say.'

'Then who should be?' snapped Benjamin in sheer frustration. 'I've been running around for weeks getting hurt, risking my life and I hardly know what I'm doing!' Benjamin stared at Jeems, who was looking down sadly into the fire. 'Gideon should be here,' Benjamin said and sighed deeply. 'He should be telling me, shouldn't he?

Benjamin thought it best to say no more. His face and hands were covered in dirt, his hair was full of sand and rock dust but most of all he was exhausted. Jeems looked up at him kindly.

'If there's one thing I know, it's that Gideon would never put anyone in danger fer no good reason.' He raised his hand to silence Benjamin and carried on. 'Yeah, meetin' up with Khor was bad. But who do ya think put those knockers in the mountains?'

Benjamin looked around. 'What knockers?'

'Well, ya said ya heard a knockin' sound, didn't ya? Just before Khor attacked us?' Benjamin felt his cheeks get hot at Jeems' raised voice.

'Yeah,' responded Benjamin nervously. 'But I don't -'

'But nothin'.' Jeems' answers were quicker now. His usual dozy self had gone. 'Those were knockers, they were. They live in mountains and have one job – ter warn people 'bout bad things lurkin' nearby.'

'Really?'

'I'm convinced of it,' Jeems responded. 'And there ain't no'un in Meridia with enough power ter call on those little guys but Gideon.' Jeems stopped to think and then nodded his head. 'I reckon he had a feelin' that we'd be meetin' up against that Khor, so he called on the Knockers ter warn us. It was me job ter notice sooner, so if anybody let ya down, I did.'

Benjamin opened his mouth to tell Jeems that he didn't let him down, but Jeems continued talking.

'Now, I don't know exactly why, but this here's the path he's got ya goin' on. And I'm only ter happy ter go it with ya. But I won't hear a word against Gideon – not a word.'

Benjamin was silent for a long time. He didn't really know what to say. He was flustered, and for a moment even wondered if being back at Hadley Priest would be better than where he was right now. Benjamin thought back to what Gideon had said to him in Water's Hyde about learning things along the way, and how difficult times make you grow. He hadn't felt as though he had grown very much, but he had got bruised and cut along the way.

As the night wore on Benjamin told Jeems a few jokes Marcus had told him, although they were quite rude and he had never been allowed to say them to an adult before. Jeems taught Benjamin a song that his mother used to sing to him when he was a baby, although he didn't let Benjamin know how long ago that was. All in all they settled down for the night, and with Primrose breathing on the fire every so often, Benjamin drifted off into a warm sleep with soft dreams of Riley snoring and Marcus tricking Hester into going outside in her dressing gown and curlers.

12

House of Stone

Benjamin and Jeems spent a further two days climbing up the mountain pass to Er's house. Still sore from their battle with Khor, they walked very slowly. Benjamin was getting tired of seeing rocks, so was quite happy when in the morning of the third day Jeems announced that they were just about at Er's.

'By noon we'll have reached the valley where Er's house is,' said Jeems.

Jeems enjoyed telling Benjamin the layout of the land and where all the paths led to. And he always seemed to know how long it would take them to get anywhere or do anything. 'With any luck, we'll have the league by sundown.'

Benjamin secretly hoped that getting the league was going to be easier than crossing the bog or climbing the mountain. But for some reason he had a very uneasy feeling about it.

'So, do you think we'll have any more, er, *things* trying to stop us?' Benjamin asked Jeems as they trudged on along the path. Quite steep at the start, the path had evened out and walking had got easier.

'Hard ter say,' Jeems said after a minute. 'No'un's ever tried ter cross Wyldewych that I know of. An' then o' course there's Er's back garden, which I imagine is full o' garden critters twice our size.'

To Benjamin, it didn't sound hopeful. Normally Benjamin wasn't at all frightened of garden creatures, but when they were bigger than him – well, that was something else. He hadn't forgotten what Gideon had said to him about the obstacles that lay ahead, and that filled his mind with thoughts of getting eaten by a gigantic snail or ladybird.

Suddenly Jeems stopped dead and Benjamin, who hadn't noticed, ran into him.

They were standing in a dip between two huge mountains at the top of a valley. In the valley below was a massive stone house with acres of fields and gardens. Along the back of the field were rows upon rows of plants and other weeds. An enormous tree was standing beyond the fields at the furthest point of the valley. Its branches were thick and bare, and it looked as though it was dying.

'Is that the Vie tree?' Benjamin asked, pointing in its direction. Jeems nodded.

'And all the stuff in front of it?'

'That's Wyldewych.' Jeems replied, pushing his pack higher up his back.

Benjamin looked at the mass of tangled weeds for a moment longer before he followed Jeems down the mountain. 'It doesn't look scary,' he said.

'In Meridia, it's the things that don't look so bad that are the worst,' Jeems responded as they trudged down.

Jeems' voice was quieter than usual. 'They say that nothin' and no'un has ever been able ter get over Wyldewych alive. Well, no'un except Gideon.' Jeems pointed to Benjamin's staff.

'Well, maybe the tree knows I'm coming,' muttered Benjamin to Jeems as they began to make their way down the hill. 'I mean, look what my staff can do and that's only one branch. Maybe it could help me get across Wyldewych.'

'Heh heh,' Jeems chortled, 'that tree's hardly bin able ter help itself fer ages. It's that bad here in Meridia, Magh and her lot killin' everythin'. It's more like yer goin' in ter try and help *it*.'

Benjamin thought hard before telling Jeems about his dream. 'The other night – well, a while ago, I guess, I had a dream about a big tree. It was as big as that Vie tree but it was alive. Lots of animals were eating from it and people were around and -'

Jeems chuckled and shook his head, causing Benjamin to stop talking. 'That tree has been like that fer as long as I can remember. Ya may have had a dream about a big tree that looked like it – but it wasn't that tree.'

'Yeah, you're probably right,' said Benjamin, shrugging his shoulders.

Although Benjamin thought the climb up the mountain was hard, he soon realised the climb down to the valley was no easier. The rock was very loose and easily dislodged, meaning a tumble down the rest of the valley. It didn't help that Jeems was very anxious about any falling rock alerting Er that they were there. As a result, much of the climb down was done in a very wide zigzag pattern that took forever.

Jeems was so worried about Er that he made Primrose stay at the top of the mountain in a large crevice until nightfall. At first Benjamin thought Jeems was just trying to scare him, but when he suggested they stop at the first sign of a good hiding place, Benjamin knew he was serious. Jeems had always made Benjamin trudge on no matter how tired he was. Despite everything they'd been through, Benjamin had never seen Jeems any other way but relaxed. Although always alert, Jeems never let on to Benjamin that he was the least bit concerned about what they were heading into. Until now.

'Why are we stopping so soon?' Benjamin asked. Jeems had led them into a small cave in the mountain face with a very low ceiling.

Jeems sat down at the mouth of the cave and looked out over the valley, his back to Benjamin.

'Cause we're down 'bout half way and I don't want ter take the chance of ol' Er sniffin' us out.' Jeems spoke to Benjamin out of the side of his mouth, his eyes never leaving the trees or the valley below.

'But we're still up so high, he'll never see us up here. Not from way down there.'

'Well, it may be *way down there* ter ya,' Jeems replied harshly. 'But ter a twenty foot giant it's a great lot closer. That, and I know he likes ter have a trek through them trees, collectin' fire wood and critters fer his tea.'

Just as Jeems finished talking some of the tree tops at the bottom of the valley started to sway. Birds rose up in protest and took flight as tree after tree was uprooted in front of Benjamin's eyes. In the small opening left by the uprooted trees, Benjamin could see the top of Er's head, his bald head piercing through the green blanket of treetops, a dull thump sounding through the valley with every step he took.

Jeems and Benjamin watched as Er strode back to his house, with no less than five full size trees cradled in his arms and a deer dangling from his fingertips.

'He's massive,' breathed Benjamin.

'And nasty,' whispered Jeems, as though the giant was standing a few feet in front of them. 'However nasty ya thought Khor was, this one's nastier. An' this one's not clumsy like Khor. He's quick and agile – he could pick up a toothpick if he wanted. Don't let his size fool ya.'

Benjamin searched for his flask of bogwash, desperate for a drink.

'We won't have a fire,' said Jeems, turning away from the entrance of the cave and laying out his bed roll. 'He's in

124

the house fer the rest o' the night, but I don't want ter risk it. Once Primrose comes down, we'll get through the trees during nightfall while he's sleepin'. Best try and get some sleep now. Yer gonna need it.' And with that Jeems turned over and went to sleep.

Benjamin found it impossible to sleep in the late afternoon, and lay awake staring at the opening of the cave with Jeems snoring in the background. He passed the time by thinking about Riley and Marcus. He hoped that they were able to stay clear of Motley since they saw him at the cellar door. The picture of Motley going right through the front door had stayed with him, and he felt prickles go up his neck and cheeks. He thought back to Marcus and Riley and some of the dreams he had of them. How they were so vivid and detailed. They seemed so real, like he was actually back at Hadley Priest. His mind turned on to the dream he'd had about the tree. Maybe it was the Vie tree after all? It wasn't always dead, was it?

Every now and then Jeems' loud snoring would snap Benjamin out of his thoughts and back to the cave. It wasn't long before dusk fell and the soft flap of Primrose's wings was heard.

Jeems was up like a shot the minute he heard Primrose, and they quickly left the safety of their mountainside shelter and headed down towards the wooded valley.

Darkness fell fast and it was only by the light from Primrose's eyes that Benjamin and Jeems could see at all. Because of their size, Benjamin had never thought that dragons could walk very fast, but Primrose proved him wrong.

'Ow!' Benjamin heard Jeems' strained voice through the darkness, followed by the sound of stumbling feet and rustling underbrush. 'That's the third root I've tripped on because that ruddy dragon won't stay with us. Primrose! Get yer dragon butt back here so we can see where we're goin'.'

Primrose came back, tail between her legs. She knew by the sound of Jeems' voice that he was not happy. And to show it he made a makeshift lead with Benjamin's rope and hung it around the dragon's neck.

'There,' he said in a satisfied voice, 'that'll keep ya close.'

Jeems gave the rope one last tug to make sure that it wasn't about to come undone. He gazed into Primrose's eyes, which had welled up with tears.

'Aw, c'mon ol' girl, don't get like that. We need yer eyes ter see, darlin'. I knows yer just excited ter go prancin' through the woods.' Jeems stroked Primrose's nose, bringing his head close to hers. 'There's a good girl. Let's go.'

Jeems rolled his eyes in Benjamin's direction, making him giggle. Primrose set out with the two following behind, Jeems holding the lead loosely in his right hand.

Jeems motioned to the lead. 'She don't really need it,' he said to Benjamin. 'But the fact that she thinks she's in trouble does it fer her everytime. She's a sensitive one, she is. Not like most dragons,' Jeems said affectionately.

'I thought dragons were really scary and mean,' replied Benjamin anxiously. The dark had always made Benjamin feel uneasy, and even being with a dragon did little to help ease that fear.

'Most of 'em are,' Jeems replied, climbing over a huge tree that had fallen down. 'But not Primrose, she's different.'

Jeems stopped talking and they walked on for another hour until Jeems pulled on Primrose's lead to get her to stop.

Jeems' voice had suddenly gone to a whisper again, and the worried tone in his voice came back.

'We're comin' in to the other end o' the woods, where Er spends most of his time. We'll look fer a place ter stop and rest while we plan our next move.'

Looking around, Benjamin could see that Jeems was right. There were huge holes where Er had uprooted trees for his fireplace, and unlike the deeper part of the woods, there were very few animals grazing about.

'He sure has taken out a lot of trees,' commented Benjamin, looking down into a huge hole in the ground. As tall as him and twice as wide if he were to lie in it, the holes were craggy and deep.

'He don' care 'bout the woods, does he? All he cares 'bout is keepin' himself warm and fed,' remarked Jeems, as he unpacked some food and tossed some over to Benjamin.

They ate another cold meal and spent the next hour before dawn dozing and helping Primrose get the forest chicken feathers out of her teeth.

Dawn slowly approached and the sky turned from black to bronze. Up ahead, Er's garden was beginning to show itself to them. Standing massively off to the left side was the giant's stone house. The house stood at least as high as a ten storey building, and looked like a pile of huge boulders stacked one on top of each other in the shape of a circle. It was almost as long as it was wide, with different heights. A huge wooden door filled the doorway, shut tight with massive hinges and a latch the size of Benjamin.

'How does he live in that pile of rock?' asked Benjamin, puzzled.

'Those boulders have been hollowed out,' Jeems replied, crouching down behind a tree and looking out to the garden.

'That's impossible,' retorted Benjamin. 'You can't hollow out a rock, especially ones that size!'

'Well, he did it, awright,' replied Jeems. 'Some reckon he picked a hole in the boulder, lifted them up an' blew the insides out like an egg.'

'I don't get it,' challenged Benjamin. 'Why did he do all that? If he wanted to live in rocks, why didn't he just find a cave in the mountains somewhere?'

'Because Er's not like other giants. He agreed to protect the league from the likes of us gettin' it. And seein' as this is where the league is, then this is where Er is.'

'But I still don't get it,' prodded Benjamin. 'Instead of trying to stop us, why didn't Magh or whoever wants the league just get it themselves?'

'Because she'd have ter go up against Gideon. And there ain't no use fightin' Gideon because no'un can beat him.'

'So why doesn't Gideon just get the leagues?' Benjamin asked impatiently.

Jeems turned to look at Benjamin, his hands on his hips. 'Where have ya bin fer the past few weeks? Wot d'yer think ya had to go into the bog and raise the oracle fer? Only you can do it, Benjermin. Yer the one, the beacon. Yer the only one that can get them out.'

'So it's all up to me,' Benjamin said soberly and walked by Jeems towards the edge of the valley.

Jeems nodded in a sullen manner. 'We best get started. Er will be awake soon and, believe me, if we can get this done without him noticin' it'll be all the better.'

The plan was to run across the field of grass towards the house and have Primrose fly over Wyldewych to the Vie tree to distract anything that might be waiting for them. Then

129

Benjamin and Jeems would make their way on foot. Once they got to the tree Benjamin would climb up and, assuming they hadn't been seen, the hard part would be done.

If it were only that easy.

13

The Garden of Er

Going across the field to Er's house proved more difficult than either Benjamin or Jeems had anticipated. The blades of grass were long and stood at least chin height to both of them. They were also heavy with early morning dew. They hadn't gone far through the field before they were drenched from the shoulders down.

They floundered out of the grass and on to the pebbled path beside the giant's house. They were soaked to the skin, their robes clinging around them, sticky and heavy.

'We can't go on like this,' Jeems whispered, trying to wring out his cloak. 'Our clothes need dryin'. Primrose! Come down 'ere an' help us out, would ya.'

Primrose flew down and landed in front of Jeems. She opened her mouth and took a deep breath when she was interrupted by a shout from Benjamin.

'Stop!'

Primrose stopped short and shot sparks across the path, but not before she got a bad case of the hiccups. Jeems whipped his head around to look at him.

'Are ya mad? Do ya want ter wake up Er, his dog Shuck an' all?'

Benjamin stood uneasily, watching Jeems' bewildered look. Primrose had her hands over her mouth and was hiccupping silently, smoke rings rising out of her nostrils.

'She was going to set you on fire,' Benjamin exclaimed.

'No she was not,' Jeems retorted, shaking his head from side to side. 'She was just goin' ter breathe a little hot air on me – ter dry me clothes. Don't be daft.' Jeems shook his head slightly and turned back to Primrose. 'Now look. Ya've gone an' given her hiccups.' Jeems watched Primrose for a moment, studying the smoke rings rising above her. 'Well, I'll take me chances. But if she does set me on fire 'cause of her hiccups it'll be yer fault.'

After his scolding from Jeems, Benjamin was sullen and silent. Even when it was his turn to have his clothes dried, he just shut his eyes tightly without uttering a single word. His hair, which had grown since being in Meridia, blew slightly in the warm breeze coming from Primrose's mouth.

Once dry, Jeems motioned Benjamin over to the pebbled path that led them in between Er's house and what looked like a garden shed. The house had looked big enough from the top of the mountain, but now that Benjamin was standing beside it he realised how enormous it was. He stepped back, scaling it with his eyes, his head raised as high up as it could when he was poked by Jeems. Jeems pointed to the other side of the path to the building that Benjamin thought was a garden shed. Looking at it again, he noticed what it really was.

132

Sound asleep, his head eye level to Benjamin, was the biggest dog he had ever seen. Dark brown in colour, with a barbed wire collar around its huge neck, the dog's head covered almost the entire opening of its house. Its snout was slightly pushed in and its jowls were droopy, with drops of drool dripping from the sides, making enormous puddles on the ground. Twitching slightly with its paws tucked under its chin, Benjamin thought it almost looked cute. It stirred slightly and crinkled its nose, exposing a huge fang from beneath its top lip.

Jeems shook his head and mouthed to Benjamin, 'Don't wake him up.' Benjamin nodded his agreement, and slowly followed Jeems past the giant sleeping dog and into the back garden.

Benjamin thought that nothing could surprise him anymore, but he stopped in his tracks at his first sight of Er's garden. Weeds and tall plants lined the garden borders that also housed rain barrels and a potting shed. Everything Benjamin saw, from the grass to the ladybirds to the dead flowers was gigantic, standing at least twice his height. Due to the length of the grass, Benjamin couldn't see very far in front of him but standing off in the distance at the end of the garden he could see the top of the Vie tree.

Jeems picked up a stick and was just about to draw a diagram of the plan in the dirt when a huge squawk broke the silence of the early morning. Startled, Jeems threw the stick in

133

the air. Benjamin jumped, sending pebbles flying in all directions and Primrose gave a very loud snort. They all looked up towards where the sound came from.

A huge black raven, much like the one Benjamin had seen at the Bogwump camp was perched on top of a potting shed, glaring down at the three of them. Jeems' eyes narrowed with anger.

'Bave,' he hissed through gritted teeth.

The raven swung his neck upwards as if to respond to his name. It ruffled its huge black feathers, puffed out its chest and opened his mouth.

'He's gonna do it again,' said Jeems. 'He's tryin' ter wake up Er's dog, Shuck. He's offerin' us up as bait. I'll have him, I will.'

Before Benjamin knew what was happening, Jeems had picked up the stick he had thrown and jumped on to a huge rain barrel that was beside the potting shed.

'Primrose, give me some snuff!' Jeems called out. Primrose immediately ran over to Jeems and with a quick puff the stick burst into flames like a matchstick. Jeems held it with both hands, struggling to steady himself on the barrel. With a loud grunt Jeems swung the blazing torch towards the raven, setting its tail feathers on fire.

The raven squawked in pain and flew towards the mountainside, its tail blazing, before dropping into a crevice and out of sight.

Benjamin heard it before he saw it. The sound of scratching claws against stone, the deep low growl and then the thunderous barking. Shuck was awake. Dead or alive, the raven had done its job.

Jeems and Benjamin exchanged a fearful look.

'RUN! HIDE! PRIMROSE, DISTRACT THAT OVERGROWN THUG!' Jeems bellowed.

Benjamin ran around the garden in a panic, trying to find a place to hide. His eyes landed on some gigantic broken flower pots nestled almost behind Shuck's house. Thinking it would be too close to danger for Shuck to find him, he raced towards them and squeezed through a crack. Once safe, he looked out to see where Jeems and Primrose were.

Primrose was flying around Shuck's gigantic head. Shuck was pawing and jumping at Primrose, his jaws clamping shut at her heels. Benjamin noticed Jeems duck down behind the rain barrels and out of sight. He continued to watch as Primrose kept flying around Shucks' head, dodging his jaws of steel.

'Get outta there, Primrose.' Primrose turned to Jeems' voice coming from behind the barrels. With Primrose distracted, Shuck's right paw slammed hard against her back leg, sending the little dragon into a tail spin and back into a bunch of huge Venus flytraps. Instantly, the flytrap opened its jaws and snapped shut around the dragon. Primrose was gone.

'No,' Benjamin said out loud.

Benjamin saw Jeems climb out from behind the barrels and start across the grass to the carnivorous plants, but something made him stop dead in his tracks. The ground was shaking. A rumble was coming from inside the house. The door swung open and out came Er.

For a moment Jeems stood frozen in his tracks. Quickly coming to his senses, he retreated to his hiding place, just barely avoiding Shuck who was bounding away from the flytraps and towards his master.

'You's makin' all dis racket? Yer dumb 'ound?'

His voice was deep and his speech sloppy. His lips were fat, round and almost the same colour as his bald head. His deep black eyes were the size of teacups.

He lumbered out of his house, his dog jumping up and whining around his knees. The ground groaned under his weight. A linen tunic stretched over his big belly. Poking from underneath his round stomach was a belt made out of deer hide. His hands, the size of dinner plates, were distinguishable only by four thick fingers and a stubby thumb, sausage-like and tight. His brown trousers were torn and sheared just below the knee.

He came out towards the garden. By the time he was standing at the cracked pots Benjamin was hiding in, all that could be seen of Er was one huge foot covered with a slipper that matched his deer hide belt.

Shuck bounded towards the rain barrel, leapt up on it and growled fiercely, his tail wagging. He went back and forth to Er, coaxing his master to come and see what he had found.

'Wha' yer got, manky mutt?' Er crossed the grass slowly. 'Not anudder of 'em ruddy ravens. Dhey've bin 'round fer de past free days.'

The hair on the back of Benjamin's neck stood on end as he watched Er approach Jeems' hiding place. At the same time he felt something press against his head and looked up to find himself eye to eye with a gigantic snail that was stuck to the top of the pot. It looked down at him with antennae-like eyes, slime dripping from the top of the pot. The slime was thick and narrowly missed Benjamin, who moved out of the way. As he looked out towards Er again, another snail was slowly crossing the path and blocking his view, leaving a sticky trail of slime behind it.

'Move,' Benjamin said, to little effect.

Benjamin jumped up and down to look over the snail. Er was moving the barrel next to where Jeems was hiding. Benjamin only had a split second to think and he knew he had to do something.

Taking a deep breath, Benjamin ran out from his hiding place, waving his arms and yelling.

'Hey! Hey! Over here!' Benjamin called out.

Er and Shuck turned their attention towards him. Er raised his huge arm and pointed. 'Hey! Yer not s'pposed ter be 'ere.' He slurred loudly. His face bore a mean frown and his thick eyebrows burrowed together into the middle of his forehead.

As Benjamin turned to run his foot slid in the slick trail of slime the snail had left and he fell face first. Benjamin pushed himself up with his hands – the whole front part of his body in pain. Smoke rose from his skin and started to bubble. He stood there staring at his hands, screaming. What was happening to him? He could smell his hair burning, could feel his skin getting hotter and hotter.

He felt Er pick him up by his collar and carry him over to the barrel full of water. He opened his eyes and tried without success to focus on the giant who was examining him closely.

'Dhat slime's poison,' commented Er gruffly. 'Too bad.'

Er plunged Benjamin into the barrel. He wanted to struggle but he couldn't. His skin felt like it was peeling off. Just when he thought that Er was going to drown him, he was lifted up and out of the water. Benjamin could make out the fuzzy outline of Er's pear-shaped face and wide, round nose. He struggled as Er brought Benjamin towards his open mouth, full of teeth. He clung onto the giant's thick finger as Er tried to shake him off and into his open mouth directly below.

Benjamin could hold on no longer and he fell into the cavernous gaping hole of the giant's mouth.

14

Tooth Decay

Benjamin's eyelids fluttered. He emitted a low, deep moan and unfolded his scorched body that he had curled in a ball. His nose crinkled at the foul smell of the shallow liquid he was in, gently sloshing back and forth.

Struggling to sit up, Benjamin studied the greyish walls of his tomb. He rested against the uneven, smooth sides and let out a small sigh of relief that he was alive. He looked up and saw a small sliver of light that was just bright enough to show him the walls were at least twice his height. He stood up and stumbled around bits of food, crunched bones and puddles of something thick and black. His battered and weary legs struggled to hold him up so he sat back down and looked at his hands.

Although very red, bruised and sore, Benjamin was both surprised and relieved to see that he had not burned his skin off. He curled his knees into his chest and began to wonder exactly where he was. A lump in his throat formed as he wondered what had become of Primrose and Jeems. His eyes stung and his bottom lip trembled. In his mind he went over how Jeems acted when he saw the raven and how he had called it by name. Jeems knew everything there was to know about Meridia, so why did he get so angry at that raven he called

Bave? What did it all mean? The last thing he remembered was Er putting him in his mouth. He wiped a tear from his cheek and closed his eyes. All he could do was wait for Er to decide his fate.

'Benjermin.'

Convinced he had just heard Jeems' voice, Benjamin opened his eyes and looked around. He strained to listen but all he could hear was a monotonous rumble above him.

'Benjermin.' The voice, definitely Jeems', was in his head again. Elated, Benjamin got up and looked around for the pork pie hat.

'Hello? Jeems? Where are you?'

'Shh! Keep yer voice down! He'll hear ya.' Jeems' voice was clearer this time. Benjamin continued to look around.

'Where – where are you? I can't see you,' said Benjamin, barely able to contain his excitement.

'I'm outside. Ya can't see me, so stop movin' around.'

Benjamin looked up. 'Then how can I hear you?'

Jeems laughed quietly. 'I may not be Gideon, but I can do a thing or two if I set me mind ter it. Grand ter hear yer voice, mate. I've bin tryin' ter get an answer outta ya fer ages.'

'Where is Er?' asked Benjamin. 'And where am I? The last thing I remember Er was trying to eat me. Has he, I mean … eaten me?'

'Er's here in the back garden, passed out on his hammock, snoring like a wild dog. And he hasn't eat'n ya yet, mate. I saw him put ya in one o' his teeth.'

'How did I –'

'No time fer questions,' Jeems cut in. 'We've gotta get ya outta there – an' fast. I reckon Er will be wakin' up soon ter go an' get summat ter eat. He's probably already fergotten about ya and will just keep ya in there ter be gnashed up with his next meal.'

Benjamin gulped. He didn't know how many more times he could deal with almost dying. 'I don't want to be chewed up,' he pleaded to Jeems.

Jeems' voice came through again. 'Don't panic on me now. Can ya climb out on yer own?'

'I don't think so.' Benjamin stood up and felt the high, smooth walls. It's too smooth and I can't reach the top. I've lost my pack and–'

'Don't worry 'bout that, I've got it.' Jeems interrupted again. 'Do ya still have the Arcrux? Is it still around yer neck?'

Benjamin hadn't even thought about it, and quickly put his hand to his neck. He breathed a sigh of relief. 'Yeah,' he answered.

'Good. I'm gonna throw ya down some rope. When ya get it, I need ya ter hold on tight, do ya hear?'

Benjamin nodded.

'Do ya hear me?' Jeems asked again.

'Oh, yeah,' Benjamin answered. 'Sorry, I forgot you couldn't see me.'

Benjamin wondered how Jeems was going to get a rope to him without waking up Er. Even if Er stayed asleep, Shuck was bound to be about, especially since he knew that Jeems was behind that barrel. Benjamin was so deep into these thoughts he didn't notice the swishing noise above him, mostly hidden amongst Er's snores.

Benjamin felt something graze the side of his face. Looking up, he noticed the rope Gideon had given him dangling inches from his nose. Benjamin heard Jeems again. 'Benjermin, slip through the loop I made in the rope an' tigh'en it up 'round yer waist. Hold on tight, it'll be a quick ride up.' Benjamin did what Jeems said and held on tight. He just had time to wrap his hands around the rope when he heard Jeems again.

'Okay, here we go.'

Benjamin's head snapped back as he was shot upwards towards daylight. Breezing past the rest of Er's molars, Benjamin looked down to see the opening of the giants' vast throat. He gripped the rope tighter.

A thud and sudden head pain followed as Benjamin's head struck the back of Er's front teeth. The force made the rope taut, knotting it around his waist even tighter. It was also enough to wake up the giant.

Er's eyes fluttered and his mouth opened into a wide yawn. Benjamin soared upwards and out of the giant's mouth, passing right by Er's open eyes.

Er's surprise was short-lived. Letting out a huge roar, Er called for Shuck and tried to leap out of his hammock but his legs got caught up and he fell to the ground. Benjamin saw Shuck stumble as the ground shook from Er's fall.

'Benjermin, up here!'

Benjamin looked up. Jeems was waving to him from the back of a white winged horse.

'Hagar?' Benjamin said.

'Don't ask me how she knew we needed her,' said Jeems. 'I reckon Gideon knew we needed some flyin' power.'

Benjamin smiled up at Jeems and watched Hagar's powerful wings take them through the air. She looked down and let out a loud neighing sound.

'She's sayin' 'allo,' Jeems said gaily and patted Hagar's neck.

After a few moments Jeems peered over Hagar to talk to Benjamin again. 'Okay, we're gonna be goin' over Wyldewych. I'm gonna throw yer staff down fer ya. Hagar an' I'll be dodgin' stuff up here, but the only thing that can knock 'em down is yer staff. Just swat like mad and ya should be fine. Once we're near the tree, jump on to it.' Jeems' voice was loud and clear. He kept looking back to see Shuck running aimlessly around Er, who was still trying to untangle himself.

Benjamin caught the staff in both hands and looked down, not sure of how he was going to fight swinging from the rope as wildly as he was. The ride was rough as Hagar dodged huge dragonflies, ladybirds and mean-looking wasps. Benjamin looked back to Er who had clambered out of his tangled hammock and was heading towards them at full speed with Shuck in tow.

'Jeems, Er is coming,' yelled Benjamin. He saw Jeems' head turn around and nod. Jeems turned back to face the front and then down at Benjamin.

'The worst is just ahead. It's up ter ya now. We'll steer ya ter were ya need ter get to, but ya've got ter do the rest by yerself.'

Benjamin nodded numbly and raised his legs from a near miss by a thorned vine that had shot upwards to grab hold of his ankle. He looked down in time to see two huge spiders leap at him from a black branch. Their pincers clicked ferociously and they spat as they darted towards Benjamin.

'Swing now, Benjermin! Hit 'em!'

Benjamin let loose on the spiders and knocked them squarely between the eyes with his staff, sending them hurtling down to the ground in front of Shuck. One spider lay motionless, but the dog yelped in fright as the other spider struggled frantically to flip off its back. Benjamin turned his

144

head just in time to see a swarm of equally large locusts heading right for him.

At least twenty of them raced towards Benjamin. The noise was deafening as they swarmed around him. He swung his staff back and forth, knocking some clear across the garden to the other side of the house.

'Benjermin, the rope! They're eatin' through the rope.' Benjamin heard Jeems scream from above and looked up. Two locusts had perched themselves on the rope and were trying to chew their way through it. Benjamin tried to swat them with his staff but he couldn't reach them. They continued munching, and Benjamin was surprised that they hadn't eaten right through already. He looked at the rope closely and remembered what Gideon said. Benjamin started to laugh.

'Yeah, go on. Stay there all day if you like, you'll never get through it.' The locusts then turned their attention to Benjamin and started coming down the rope, gritting their razor sharp teeth. With two swings of his staff they were knocked down in to a puddle of water that hissed and smouldered and sucked the locusts under. Jeems whooped and cheered as they continued on towards the tree.

Benjamin knocked away a poisonous snail that was being carried by a fly with the face of a goblin and two human-like arms. He looked down and saw the same type of faces on loads of little fiends running throughout Wyldewych. They climbed on every twisted branch, throwing spiky rocks, beetles and anything else they could find.

'Ah,' Benjamin cried as he felt something pierce his right arm. He looked to see a spiky rock stuck in his flesh. Almost immediately the rock sprouted four legs, three eyes and eight of the largest fangs he had ever seen. It began scurrying towards him, menacing and vicious.

High above, Jeems and Hagar were having problems of their own, as some of the little winged goblins were flying around Jeems, threatening to carry him away. Hagar was batting away some with her hooves, sending them back down into Wyldewych. Benjamin tried to swat the rock beetle on his arm with his left hand but only hit one of the many spikes on its back, causing a gash across the palm of his hand. It was up to Benjamin's shoulder before Jeems noticed.

'Hagar, Benjermin's in trouble, swing to the right.' Hagar made a sharp right turn, enabling Benjamin to switch his staff to his other hand. The staff connected to the teacup-sized beetle which was sent flying as it was about to sink its front fangs into Benjamin's neck.

'Benjermin, hang on!'

Jeems' warning was none too soon. Benjamin had just gained a good hold on his staff again as Hagar folded in her wings and went into a death roll dive to avoid the swarm of bright red dragonflies that were coming down on them. Benjamin twisted and turned at a nauseating speed until Hagar straightened out. While Benjamin was getting over his dizziness, a dragonfly with teeth and a forked tongue bit his arm before he could stop it. The pain brought tears to his eyes, but he kept swinging and, one by one, the dragonflies fell into Wyldewych.

'Benjermin, look ahead,' Jeems called.

Benjamin looked up and noticed the Vie tree up ahead. He struggled to loosen the rope around his waist, but his hands were cut and bleeding and the rope was really tight.

'I'll git cha,' Er's voice boomed across to where Benjamin was swinging from Hagar. Er had finally freed himself from his hammock and was gaining on them. Benjamin kept looking up to where Er was while he continued to struggle with the rope. His hands burned with pain and they were covered in blood from the gashes. He looked up again. Er was close, almost within arm's reach. He looked down again at Wyldewych racing past. Hagar was going faster to keep ahead of Er but was making it difficult to see the ground.

'Benjermin! You need to jump now, Hurry!'

Jeems was like a distant voice breaking through the rumble of the giant and his dog. Benjamin looked over his shoulder - Er's fingertips were almost touching him. All of the Wyldewych goblins cheered for the giant as he swiped at Benjamin's arm. Shuck jumped intermittedly, clamping his jaws inches away from Benjamin's feet. Benjamin's hands trembled with panic. His slippery hands couldn't loosen the tight rope.

The Arcrux swung from Benjamin's neck as they flew over the Vie tree. With one final attempt, Benjamin's hands untied the knot that was restraining him. He jumped and landed on a branch midway down the side of the Vie tree. As he jumped, he felt Er barely miss him with another swipe.

Benjamin looked for Jeems. He was still astride Hagar and was headed towards Er. Er howled as Hagar used her back legs to kick at his head and neck.

Inch by inch, Benjamin climbed up towards the centre of the tree, looking for the hole in the trunk that was lined with gold. There were many knots and holes that had been dug by wood beetles and other animals, but none of them had a gold lining. He strained forward, his body in agony and his hands still bleeding heavily.

Benjamin was suddenly thrown off balance and had to grab on to a branch to keep from falling off. Er had got to the tree and shook it violently to dislodge Benjamin. The tree groaned deeply and millions of thorns sprang out all over its trunk and branches. Er wailed as he was struck deep in the hands and arms by the thorns. Shuck was inside Wyldewych, yelping and trying to dodge the goblins. Benjamin wove through the thorns and crawled on his belly towards the top where he could see a faint glow. At last he reached the hole and peered in – the gold almost blinded him.

The hole, although quite big, was not nearly wide enough for Benjamin to fit, small though he was. He called out to Jeems, circling overhead on Hagar.

'Jeems! The hole is too small,' Benjamin called out franticly.

'What.' Jeems responded impatiently. 'Whadda ya expect, it's a tree. Just jump in, ya'll fit – and hurry!'

Not wasting another minute, Benjamin lunged into the hole head first and slid down through the tree. He landed with a thud on the soft springy ground, the roots of the trees all around him.

'Now what?' Benjamin said to himself as he stood up. He tried to think about what Thuglot and Gideon had told him.

He got to his knees and began to dig when he was knocked off balance again. Chopping sounds came from the other side of the trunk as Er got started to cut the tree down with an axe. Benjamin regained his balance and crawled back to where he had been, digging with all his strength. He scratched and clawed at the roots to find the seed pod, the tree shaking with every chop.

He continued to dig, despite being knocked about by Er, who was too close for comfort. He felt something hard and dense, like clay.

This can't be the way, thought Benjamin, wiping the sweat off his brow.

Just then he came to a hard chunk of dirt the size of a golf ball. He broke it and found three little seeds. He fumbled with the Arcrux and tried to open one of the chambers, but it wouldn't budge. He tried another, and another, until he managed to open the one that was labelled 'E'. He carefully placed the seeds in and closed it. The Arcrux shut tight with a little snap, and he looked around frantically, trying to find a way out. He pushed the sides of the tree but they were solid. Suddenly the tree trunk above him cracked and a burst of light pierced through the darkness. Shuck's huge snout plunged in to the trunk and Benjamin was knocked aside. Er was towering over him, glaring wildly. He was talking so fast Benjamin couldn't understand a word he was saying, but it did not sound happy.

Er's gigantic hand came down, his fingers closing together to pick Benjamin up. Benjamin froze in fear and surprise. His feet dangled and he struggled wildly as he was seized by his collar.

Er laughed a sloppy laugh. He grabbed Benjamin around the waist and began to squeeze. Benjamin tried to call for Jeems, but was unable to breathe. He could feel his insides being squished as Er tightened his grip. With one last burst of energy, Benjamin swung his staff at Er's hand. The blow of the staff cracked the giant's hand and he dropped Benjamin who fell towards Wyldewych.

A stretched out vine was just about to catch Benjamin when the sound of flapping wings behind him caught his attention.

'Jeems, Help!' Benjamin cried in a hoarse voice.

Then many things happened at once. Benjamin landed hard on Hagar's back as she skimmed the tops of Wyldewych to catch him, and then up through the air at top speed. The Vie tree split in two and fell to the ground. A huge cracking sound followed and the ground below Er and Shuck opened. The wind changed violently and the Vie tree collapsed into a pile of ashes. From the dust a ring of light came forth, encompassing the entire valley. Everything the light struck disintegrated in to ashes. Er and Shuck stood there stunned until they were swallowed up by the ground, with the entire valley left in ashes and dust.

Watching the Wydewych vanish from sight, Benjamin lay back on Hagar's soft back. His racing heart was starting to slow and his breathing began to even.

'I- I got it. I got the league.' Benjamin said panting between breaths. 'It's in the Arcrux. I got it.'

Benjamin lay still, his body in immense pain, his hands raw and torn. Jeems leant over him and stroked his hair.

'Yer awright now, mate. We've got ya. Sorry about the bumpy ride earlier. Look, Primrose is here an' all. That ol' venus flytrap couldn't digest her so spat her out.'

Benjamin opened his eyes again to see the diamond eyes of Primrose gazing back at him. Her snout nuzzled into him and her soft, warm tongue licked his wounds. Weakly, he put his hand on her nose and closed his eyes while they flew out of the valley.

****

The dust cleared and the sun began to set on the valley that once held Wyldewych. All that was left was a thick floor of ash. The valley was desolate, not a living thing was left.

The soft sound of footsteps disturbed the silence of the valley. The bottom of a brown cloak trailed in the ashes and stopped where the Vie tree once stood. A wrinkled hand came out from underneath the cloak and began to brush away the ash, exposing a small green seedling that unfolded inches above the ashes. Glistening green in the sunset, its tender leaves swayed gently in the breeze.

15

Up The Stairs

Benjamin sat curled in the brown velvet chair in front of the green fire at Water's Hyde. Both of his bandaged hands were cupped around a steaming cup of Horlicks and he had the blanket from his bed wrapped around him. Out of the corner of his eye he could see Gideon coming towards him.

'You're up early.'

'I can't sleep,' Benjamin said. 'Every time I close my eyes all I see is the destruction I caused.'

Gideon poured himself a cup of tea and sat down on the chair beside Benjamin. He peered at Benjamin over his half-moon spectacles and passed him a biscuit. 'What destruction is it that you think you have caused?'

Benjamin looked at Gideon in disbelief. There was no sense of sarcasm in Gideon's voice.

'The Vie tree is gone and it's because of me. If Er didn't catch me then Jeems wouldn't have had to save me. We would have been able to get the league without Er noticing and he wouldn't have chopped the tree down.' Benjamin stared hard into his drink. His eyes began to sting. He knew that Gideon was looking at him and didn't want to meet his gaze.

'The tree did not die because Er chopped it down, and Er was not swallowed by the earth because of anything you did.

153

The tree died because it was its time. You saw it for yourself, Benjamin - decrepit and defeated. It shows just how much evil had conquered the valley that even the Vie tree struggled to survive. But by getting the league into the Arcrux you defeated the darkness that was over both the tree and the valley. What you did was give the tree new life. The life it is supposed to have, not one of oppression and death. And it certainly was not intended to live amongst the likes of Wyldewych, where no beauty is found.'

'I had a dream about the Vie tree. Or so I thought it was. But it didn't look the same.' Benjamin said, playing with the end of the blanket.

Gideon looked up at the ceiling. 'How was it different?'

'It was just as big, but it had leaves all over it and people were around it.'

Gideon raised his eyebrows. 'I would suggest that your dream was about how the tree used to be.'

'It's just that – I was there too. In my dream, by the tree.' Gideon laid his eyes to rest on Benjamin. 'Then everything was destroyed. Everything, except – except me.' By the look on Gideon's face Benjamin knew he had not expected to hear that.

'Sometimes our dreams tell us of things that have happened. And sometimes they tell us of things to come.'

'So what was my dream?' Benjamin asked.

'I'm afraid, Benjamin, that is a question I cannot answer right now. But it will, I'm sure, become clearer.'

The two sat together in silence for a long time. Benjamin turned his adventures over in his mind. 'Gideon, can I ask you something?'

'You can ask me anything you want, and I will do my best to answer you.'

'Where did Er come from?'

'Er is from the mountain area of Meridia, where there used to be many giants just like him. He chose to guard the Vie tree, although I do not think he knew exactly what he was getting into.'

'And now he's gone.' Benjamin cast his eyes downwards. 'I can't help thinking that it was my fault.'

'It was Er's decision to be a servant of Magh that led to his destruction. Just as your decision to do what is right has led you here.' Gideon got up and made Benjamin another drink.

'But I didn't make the decision,' Benjamin replied. 'I didn't believe that it was supposed to be me.'

Gideon turned and looked squarely at Benjamin. 'The moment you agreed to follow me, you believed.'

After giving Benjamin his drink, Gideon turned to the hearth. When he turned back to face Benjamin, the scales were hovering over his hands. One side was only slightly heavier.

'They've moved,' said Benjamin. 'Does that mean we've done it? Does that mean we've won?'

'The scale has moved in the right direction,' answered Gideon. He brought the scales over to Benjamin. They were a deep bronze colour and teetered on a silver pole. 'Some good has been restored in Meridia, and that has only been achieved by what you have done today. By securing the Earth league into the Arcrux, we have made gains.'

'So is that it?' Benjamin asked wearily.

Gideon put the scales back on the hearth before responding. 'What we have gained today is definitely a step forward but not, I'm afraid, enough to secure the balance overall. That will only be accomplished once all of the leagues have found their way back in to the Arcrux. But it has shifted slightly in our direction, and that, Benjamin, is something to celebrate.'

Benjamin sipped his drink and listened as Jeems and Primrose snored in unison in the corner. Jeems was very tired and sore when they finally returned to Water's Hyde. Primrose was lying next to Jeems. Her right wing had broken when the Venus Flytrap first caught her in its jaws and she now had a huge bandage over it. Other than that, she looked almost unscathed.

'Well, I had loads of help,' Benjamin said looking over at his two companions. 'And Hagar – I don't know what we would have done without her.'

'Yes, Hagar does seem to have a knack for being in the right place at the right time. However, I dare say that she may have had some assistance with knowing exactly where to go.' Gideon gave Benjamin a little smile. All annoyance and anger with Gideon gone, Benjamin smiled.

'Gideon?'

'Another question?'

Benjamin laughed nervously. 'How come I'm so different here? I would have never been able to do everything I've done back at Hadley Priest. It doesn't make sense to me.'

Gideon chuckled and nodded his head slowly. 'I am sure that you have noticed by now that things in Meridia have a certain way about them. Things happen here that may never seem to happen in your world. With that I can say there are forces and powers at work in Meridia that you may not have ever seen before. Whether you are different or not, I suppose, is for you to decide. I personally think that everything you have done here is nothing more than what you have been able to do all along, but for one reason or another you have felt unable to. This has allowed people to control you and what they do to you.'

Benjamin looked intently at Gideon before dropping his eyes to the floor.

'Benjamin, you may remember when I told you that this journey would take you further than just the other side of Meridia. The strength you have shown is just what I was talking about. I am in no doubt that this will continue when you get back to Hadley Priest.'

Benjamin snapped his head towards Gideon. 'Back? I can't go back. You said there were three more leagues. You said I was the one that was supposed to stop Magh.' Benjamin's heart skipped a beat. As horrible some of his time in Meridia had been, he didn't want to go back. He felt at home in Meridia. He belonged. And he knew that he would never be able to find the other leagues from Hadley Priest.

Gideon raised his hand slightly and shook his head, 'And that is precisely what you will do, but not right now. There is little else we can do for the moment. Magh has been alerted of your presence in Meridia, and it is only a matter of time before she catches up with you. Meridia is in peril, Benjamin. There is little left on our side – but a small shift in the scales, and some time. We have more time than her right now and we need to use it to our advantage. I am sorry, but that is all I can say. The rest you will learn as you continue your journey.'

Benjamin understood only some of what Gideon was talking about, but he was too tired to figure out the rest. His whole body ached and his bandaged hands stung. He looked around Water's Hyde and thought how different it would be to be back at Hadley Priest. It would be weird to be invisible and insignificant again.

Gideon responded to Benjamin's thoughts, as if able to read his mind. 'The courage you have shown in Meridia will not leave you. That, Benjamin, is something that noone will ever be able to take away from you.'

'But what about Hester? And school? I've been gone for so long, how am I going to explain that? What am I supposed to say? And how will I ever get back here?'

'You might do well to play along with whatever explanation Hester has dreamed up. After all, she may still be slightly unsure of you.' Gideon leaned his head into Benjamin and grinned. 'Oh, and don't fret over the right time to come back. It will be as plain to you as it was the first time.'

Without another word Gideon led Benjamin down the centre corridor to the back of Water's Hyde. Gideon took the key Benjamin had found on the floor out of his pocket. 'This key is the only way to open the door between Meridia and Hadley Priest.' Gideon faced Benjamin and spoke his last words. 'Please be sure to keep both the Arcrux and the oracle with you at all times. It is very, very important that they do not fall into the wrong hands.'

'I won't let them out of my sight,' Benjamin responded. 'Say goodbye to Jeems for me?'

Gideon bowed his head.

'Tell him I'm sorry I left without saying goodbye.'

'Jeems will understand,' Gideon said kindly. 'He knows only too well the task at hand. He and Primrose will be waiting for you when you come back.'

'And what about you?' Benjamin asked.

'I will always be exactly where you left me,' Gideon answered.

Gideon winked and turned the key into the locked door in front of them. The door opened to a flight of small, steep stairs ascending into darkness. Benjamin climbed up until he reached the cellar door to Hadley Priest. He opened and closed the door quietly behind him. Moments later Hester's bedroom door opened and they were standing face to face.

For a second Hester looked shocked and unnerved to see Benjamin. But she soon brushed it off and the usual scowl came across her face. 'Where've you been for the past month?'

'Er – '

Hester must have had second thoughts because she put her hand up to stop Benjamin from saying anything. 'I don't want to know what you've been up to, actually.' She looked at him intently, but kept her distance just the same. 'So what exactly makes runaways like you come back?'

Benjamin shifted uneasily and held his trembling hands behind his back. He was just about to say something he knew was going to sound stupid when Riley came bounding down the stairs. 'Benjamin's back!' He announced with a huge grin on his face. 'Where have you been? I've got so much to tell you? Hester's been -' his voice trailed off when he noticed Hester standing inches away.

By this time Riley had pressed right in to Benjamin and was looking up at him with a smile on his face, which soon turned in to a look of disappointment. 'I took the top bunk when you left. I guess I'll go and put my stuff back down to the bottom bunk.' He started upstairs with his head slumped, but turned when he was halfway up. 'You're still going to be here when I come back down right?'

'Yeah.' Benjamin smiled.

'Promise?'

'I promise.'

Riley smiled and skipped up the rest of the stairs, only to be met by Marcus. 'See,' he whispered. 'Motley didn't kill him after all.'

Marcus came down the rest of the stairs, smiling broadly with his hands in his pockets. 'Alright?'

'Never better. And you?'

Marcus noticed Hester. 'No change.'

Hester risked coming closer. 'I'm only going to say this once so you better listen up. Don't you even think about pulling a stunt like that again - '

'Which stunt are you referring to?' Benjamin asked smugly, spurring a smirk from Marcus.

Hester didn't' reply, like she was afraid to say anything else to him, the stair incident still clearly in her mind. Without another word she brushed passed him and out the door.

Benjamin and Marcus watched her leave. 'C'mon upstairs,' Marcus said. 'Riley and I have got loads to tell you.'

Benjamin looked around before he followed along. Everything was exactly the same as before he left. Through the window, he saw Motley out of the corner of his eye, standing in the back garden. Their eyes met, and even though Benjamin could feel a chill up his spine, he was determined not to look away first. Eventually Motley turned and disappeared through the back gate.

Printed in the United Kingdom by
Lightning Source UK Ltd., Milton Keynes
139368UK00001B/131/P